JOE COLTON

There's nothing like ~~coming~~ home, *Hacienda de Alegría,* ~~~~
The entire Colton clan is coming together from far and wide to celebrate my sixtieth birthday. I worry about my kids when they aren't around, some more than others. Take my darling daughter, Sophie. I see red every time I think of anyone trying to hurt my sweet baby girl, but I'm glad she's back where she belongs. And if it means putting some distance between her and that gold-digging fiancé of hers, even better. Now, my foster son River James is a man worthy of my daughter's affections. Ever since I took this hard-edged rebel into my home, I've sensed something special brewing between those two. I don't care what either of them say to the contrary—they belong together. Just like me and my Meredith do. But things haven't been so rosy between us for a while now. However, I refuse to give up on her... or any of my own. Something tells me we have some rough times ahead....

About the Author

KASEY MICHAELS

is a *New York Times* and *USA TODAY* bestselling author of more than one hundred books that range from contemporary to historical romance. She has earned three starred reviews from *Publishers Weekly*, and has won a RITA® Award from Romance Writers of America and an *RT Book Reviews* Career Achievement Award, Waldenbooks and Bookrak awards, and several other commendations for her writing excellence. When asked about her work for THE COLTONS series, she said that she has rarely felt so involved in a project, one with such scope and diversity of plot and characters.

Kasey Michaels

Beloved Wolf

Published by Silhouette Books

America's Publisher of Contemporary Romance

Special thanks and acknowledgment are given
to Kasey Michaels for her contribution
to THE COLTONS series.

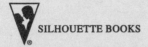 SILHOUETTE BOOKS

Recycling programs
for this product may
not exist in your area.

ISBN-13: 978-0-373-38704-5

BELOVED WOLF

Visit Silhouette at www.eHarlequin.com

Printed in U.S.A.

THE COLTONS

Meet the Coltons—
a California dynasty with a legacy of privilege and power.

Sophie Colton: *The rich girl.* This beautiful executive seemed to have it all—until her world was brutally shattered one dark night by a vicious act. Coming home to Prosperino, there's only one person to whom she can turn—the renegade she'd once loved with all her adolescent soul.

River James: *The brooding loner.* This proud Native American had once known he was all wrong for Sophie Colton—but now his heart wanted him to believe otherwise....

Joe Colton: *The honorable family patriarch.* On the eve of his sixtieth birthday, this savvy tycoon sensed something was amiss...something that could threaten the very essence of the Colton dynasty!

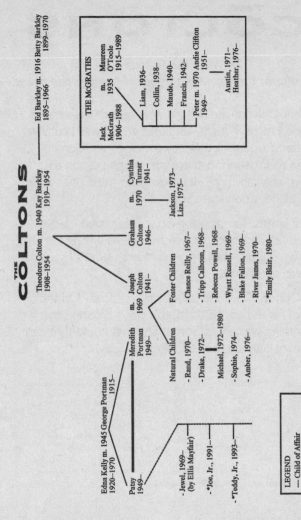

THE COLTONS

Theodore Colton m. 1940 Kay Barkley
1908–1954   1919–1954

Ed Barkley m. 1916 Betty Barkley
1895–1966   1899–1970

Edna Kelly m. 1945 George Portman
1920–1970   1915–

Meredith Portman
1949–

Patsy
1949–

m. Joseph Colton 1969 1941–

Graham Colton
1946–

m. 1970 Cynthia Turner
1941–

Jackson, 1973–
Liza, 1975–

Natural Children
- Rand, 1970–
- Drake, 1972–
- Michael, 1972–1980
- Sophie, 1974–
- Amber, 1976–

Foster Children
- Chance Reilly, 1967–
- Tripp Calhoun, 1968–
- Rebecca Powell, 1968–
- Wyatt Russell, 1969–
- Blake Fallon, 1969–
- River James, 1970–
- *Emily Blair, 1980–

- Jewel, 1969–
(by Ellis Mayfair)
- *Joe, Jr., 1991–
- *Teddy, Jr., 1993–

THE McGRATHS

Jack
McGrath
1906–1988

m.
1935

Maureen
O'Toole
1915–1989

Liam, 1936–
Collin, 1938–
Maude, 1940–
Francis, 1942–
Peter m. 1970 Andie Clifton
1949–   1951–

Austin, 1971–
Heather, 1976–

LEGEND
— Child of Affair
▬ Twins
• Adopted by Joe Colton

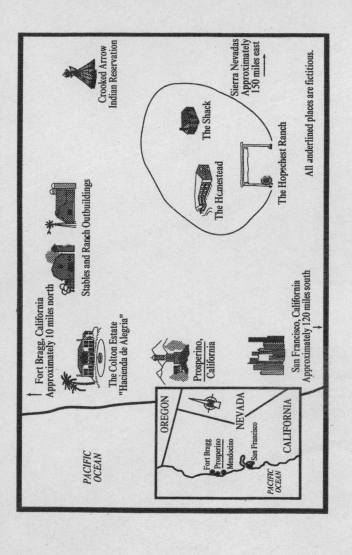

Fort Bragg, California
Approximately 10 miles north

PACIFIC
OCEAN

The Colton Estate
"Hacienda de Alegria"

Stables and Ranch Outbuildings

Crooked Arrow
Indian Reservation

The Shack

The Homestead

Sierra Nevadas
Approximately
150 miles east

The Hopechest Ranch

Prosperino,
California

San Francisco, California
Approximately 120 miles south

All underlined places are fictitious.

OREGON

NEVADA

CALIFORNIA

PACIFIC
OCEAN

Fort Bragg
Prosperino
Mendocino
San Francisco

One

Nothing, absolutely nothing, had gone right for Sophie Colton that entire early-April San Francisco day.

The new telephone system touted by her advertising agency boss to make everyone's life easier had lost her a hard-won connection with a client in Tokyo—twice—and had probably cost her an important account.

The child star who had just been signed for a national commercial had picked this week to have his voice go from angelically pure to crackly pubescent, and would have to be replaced.

She'd gotten a run in her panty hose on the way to lunch with a client, been caught in a quick shower the weather forecasters had missed, and now she'd had an argument over dinner with Chet Wallace, her fiancé since this past Christmas.

Okay. Maybe not an argument. Maybe that was too strong a word. A disagreement. She and Chet never argued. Mostly he talked and Sophie listened. Sometimes she wondered why she listened.

Chet wanted to leave their cushy jobs at the San Francisco advertising agency and strike out on their own, form their own company. Sophie wasn't so sure. She liked her job, had worked hard to get it, and in this cutthroat world, starting a marriage and a new business at the same time...well, it scared her.

At least that was what she tried to tell herself as she walked home in the dark after throwing a mini-tantrum at the restaurant and leaving Chet to finish dessert and pay the check on his own.

Maybe what really bothered her was that Chet had done just that. He'd stayed behind, sipping coffee and eating his chocolate mousse, and let her go. Granted, she lived only four blocks from the restaurant, but did he have to be so blasé about it? Tell her to take a walk, cool down, and he'd meet her at her apartment in thirty minutes? She hated Chet when he was reasonable. Didn't he know that?

Sophie stopped at the curb of an alleyway situated halfway down a long city block. She lifted her head, sighed and pushed at her chin-length golden brown hair, tucking a naturally blond-streaked lock behind her ear. She blinked her huge brown eyes that were so like her mother's, sighed again and stepped off the curb, one long straight leg in its three-inch heel making contact with the macadam...before she was suddenly being pushed, shoved back into the alleyway.

"Hey!" she called out loudly, trying to disengage

herself from the arms that held her. She was pushed against a dew-slick brick wall so hard that anything else she might have said was lost. The side of her head slammed against the bricks, and seemingly all the air in her lungs whooshed out of her body.

It was unreal. Surreal. Couldn't be happening. Certainly couldn't be happening to *her*.

But it was. As she fought to stay conscious, as she struggled to breathe, to beat down the panic that rose like bile in her throat, Sophie felt the tip of a knife press against her throat.

"Move, bitch, and I'll cut you. You got that?"

She couldn't nod. She'd be cut if she moved. So she blinked. *Yes,* that blink said silently. *I've got that.*

"Okay. Okay-okay-okay," the male voice said. Her attacker was obviously very excited, possibly high on drugs. Sophie didn't know, couldn't be sure. She just knew the man was nervous, hyper, definitely out of control. He might kill her even as he said he wouldn't.

The knife eased away from her throat, and the next thing Sophie knew she was facedown on the hard gravel in the alleyway, her right knee exploding in agony as it took the brunt of her fall.

Sophie closed her eyes against the white-hot pain and swallowed. "What—what do you want?" she managed to ask, still unable to move, for the man's knee pressed hard against her back. "I don't have a purse, but there's a wallet in my coat pocket. Money. Credit cards. Let—let me get it for you."

"Don't listen, do you, bitch? Huh, huh?" the man growled against her ear, his putrid breath and body odor turning her stomach. "Move and die, bitch, move and die."

Then his hands were on her, touching her through her light coat, for the evening had been warm, and she hadn't expected to be on the streets anyway. She could feel him brace most of his body weight on the knee jabbing into her back, while he used his left hand to reach under her, twist her upper body painfully and clumsily pinch and paw at her throat, her breasts. He bit her shoulder, hard.

Maniac. The man was a maniac. He didn't want her money—or he'd take it once she was dead. What he wanted was her. Her body. He wanted to hurt her.

She was only twenty yards from a main street, and she was helpless. He still held the knife in his right hand as he groped at her with his left. His stronger body pinned her against the gravel. If she cried out, she'd die.

Did it matter if she moved, if she fought? The man was out of his mind, out of control. He had a knife. She'd die anyway.

But she'd be damned if she'd die without a struggle.

Sophie might be a city girl now, years away from her roots on a California ranch, but she'd been a tomboy once, a girl child with big brothers she'd often fought with, sometimes in fun, sometimes in earnest.

Brothers. Oh, God. Michael had died, and his death had nearly destroyed her parents, her entire family. If she were to die, too... No! No, that couldn't happen! She wouldn't let that happen! *Mommy! Daddy! I won't let that happen!*

Forgetting the pain in her right knee, forgetting the knife blade she could feel pressing against her jawline, forgetting the violation she felt as the man's hand slipped inside her V-neck blouse, his filthy, jagged fingernails tearing at her skin, Sophie reacted.

She dug her elbows and knees into the gravel and bucked like a wild pony out to unseat the rider on its back. Fear lent her strength, and surprise gave her a second advantage. The off-balance man toppled to one side, so that she could backpedal away from him on her hands and buttocks, putting precious space between them.

"Help! *Help!*" she screamed at the top of her lungs. "In the alley. Help me!" As she screamed, Sophie grabbed on to a huge plastic garbage can and somehow got to her feet, her right leg all but useless. She pulled the top off the garbage can and threw it at the man, then blindly reached into the open can and pulled out the first "weapon" to come to hand— the sliced-off top of a pineapple.

What a ridiculous weapon. But, then, the alleyway ran behind a block of upscale restaurants. What had she expected to find, a fully loaded .357 Magnum?

Sophie threw the pineapple top at the man, followed by a huge, empty can of tomato puree and two handfuls of rotting vegetables, all the time screaming for help. She knocked over smaller, metal garbage cans, making more noise than impact, but making herself as undesirable a victim as possible. "In the alley! Help me! Help me!"

The man cursed, ducked a wilted cabbage and ran

off down the alley moments before two well-dressed men entered the alley, coming to Sophie's rescue.

"Oh, thank God," she said, falling against one of them as the other ran back toward the street to call an ambulance and the police.

Sophie's right knee hurt her so much that she didn't even know that her attacker's knife had laid open her cheek from ear to chin, that she was losing blood rapidly. She knew nothing at all, for within moments she had sunk into blessed unconsciousness.

Louise Smith sat up straight in her narrow bed, her eyes wide with fright, her body drenched in perspiration in the heat of the Mississippi night. Something was wrong. Something was very wrong.

She slipped from the bed, stumbled to the light switch, then pressed her hands against the top of the dresser, blinked at her reflection in the mirror. She saw a woman who somehow didn't look all of her fifty-two years—except for her large brown eyes, which held the misery of the ages. She ran a hand through her wavy, golden-brown hair that showed very little gray and took several deep, steadying breaths, trying to beat down the panic that still held her in its grip.

See? It's just you. Nobody else is here. Nobody can harm you. Nobody knows. Nobody. Not even you.

She'd been dreaming. She dreamed so often. All the dreams were confusing. Some of them were good, for a while, but all of them ended unhappily, with no answers, no resolution.

But this had been different. She couldn't remember

a dream. All she could remember was a flash of fright...and the certainty that she was needed, that someone needed her help.

A child. A little girl. A little girl who called her Mommy.

But where was she? Where?

Louise left her bedroom, padded toward the kitchen and a glass of water, knowing she would not be able to sleep anymore that night.

Joe Colton burst from the elevator before the doors had fully opened and raced down the corridor toward the nurse's station, his foster son River James right behind him. They'd flown from the family ranch in Prosperino, River at the controls, within an hour of the phone call from the San Francisco police, arriving shortly before dawn.

"My daughter—Sophie Colton," Joe demanded of the unit clerk, who was otherwise occupied in filing her nails. "What room is she in?"

The young woman looked up at him blankly. "Colton? I don't think we have a Colton." She swiveled in her chair, spoke to a nurse who'd just come into the station. "Mary, do we have a Colton?"

The nurse stepped forward, looking at Joe. "May I ask who you are, sir?"

"I'm her father, damn it!" Joe exploded, his large frame looking more menacing than paternal at that moment, his nearly sixty years having made small impact on him other than to dust some silver in his dark brown hair.

River took off his worn cowboy hat, put a hand on

his foster father's arm and smiled at the nurse. "Senator Colton is a little upset, ma'am," he said, being his most charming at the same time he emphasized the word *senator,* even if Joe had left office years earlier. "His daughter was mugged last evening. Colton. Sophie Colton."

It might have been the dropping of Joe Colton's title, or it might have been River's lazy smile, but Mary quickly stepped out from behind the desk, asking the two men to follow her down the corridor.

"I'm sorry, Senator," Mary said as they walked, "but your daughter was the victim of a crime. We can't be too careful. She came back from surgery a little over an hour ago and is probably sleeping, but I can tell you that she made it through the surgery without incident. Have you been apprised of her injuries?"

"Oh, God." Joe stopped, put a hand to his mouth and turned away from the nurse. Obviously the long night had taken its toll. That, River thought, and the fact that Meredith Colton, Sophie's mother, hadn't seen any reason to accompany her husband to San Francisco.

"Yes, we have, but we'd like to hear a recap from you, if you don't mind," River said, stepping up, taking over for this so very strong man who had already buried one child. River knew he couldn't understand all that Joe must have been going through since the call about Sophie had come into the ranch, but he had a pretty good idea that the man had been living in his own special hell, reliving the call about Michael, fearing the worst for his daughter.

River, however, had been more mad than frightened, once he'd spoken to the patient liaison at the hospital, who had assured him that Sophie's injuries, although extensive, were not life threatening. While Joe Colton had sat in the back of the small private jet, praying for his daughter, River had been at the controls, wishing himself in San Francisco so that he could knock down Chet Wallace. Then pick him up, knock him down again. And again.

Joe collected himself and motioned for the nurse to continue down the hallway.

"She suffered a mild concussion, Senator," Mary told them, stopping in front of Room 305, her hand on the metal door plate. "I want to prepare you for that, as she may be confused for a while once she wakes. Plus, she's got lots of scrapes and bruises, from her contact with a brick wall, as I understand it, and the gravel in the alley. Those have been cleaned up, of course. And there are some fairly deep scratches on her...on her chest. They'll be painful, but aren't serious, and we've already begun treatment with antibiotics. We can't be too careful with human bites and scratches. I—I'm sorry."

The bastard had bitten her? River hadn't known that part, wished Joe didn't have to know that part.

Joe moaned low in his throat. River squeezed his work-hard hands into fists.

Mary continued, "The orthopods put her knee back together—torn Medial Meniscus, which is fairly common—but she's in a J-brace and will be on crutches for at least five or six weeks, and then will need some pretty extensive rehab. And," she added, sighing,

"Dr. Hardy, chief of reconstructive surgery, sewed up the knife gash on her face. She'll need follow-up plastic surgery, at least that's what's on Dr. Hardy's post-op notes, but at least she's been put back together. It's a miracle the knife didn't hit any large blood vessels or nerves. Still, even though the cut wasn't dangerously deep, it took over one hundred stitches to close her up again."

"Oh, God," Joe said. "My baby. My beautiful, beautiful baby."

River clenched his teeth until his jaw hurt. Sophie. Beautiful Sophie. Dragged into an alley. Mauled, beaten, cut, damn near killed. And for no reason, no reason at all. Just because a bastard high on drugs had gone berserk. Just because she'd been in the wrong place at the wrong time. Now her entire life had been changed forever.

"I think we're prepared to see her now, ma'am," River said, motioning for the nurse to step back so that he and Joe could enter Sophie's room. "We promise not to disturb her."

"Certainly," Mary agreed, then walked past them, back to the nurse's station.

"Ready, Joe?" River asked, a hand on his foster father's back.

"No," Joe told him, his voice so low River had to lean close to hear him. "A parent is never ready to see his child lying in a hospital bed." He lifted his head and took a deep breath. "But let's do it."

River pushed open the door, let Joe precede him into the room, then followed after him. He didn't want to see Sophie this way, injured, helpless. That was not how he had seen her when he'd first come to live at the ranch and she'd chased after him until he'd let down his guard and let her into his life. His Sophie, four years his junior, which had been such a huge gap when they were younger. The angry young man and the awkward, braces-on-her-teeth, skinned-knees, pig-tailed, hero-worshiping kid.

She'd driven him crazy, made him angry. Gotten under his skin. Wormed her way into his bruised, battered and wary heart.

And then she'd grown up.

Oh, God, she'd grown up.

She'd talked him into escorting her to her high school senior prom. They'd danced, they'd talked about how she would leave the following morning to do an internship at Joe's radio station in Dallas, before she began college in the fall.

She'd kissed him. He'd kissed her back. Again and again and again. He'd held her, trying not to say the words that screamed inside his head: "Don't go, don't go. Stay with me, Sophie. Love me, Sophie."

The foster son of Joe Colton owed the man better than that. The half-breed son of a drunk owed Sophie more than that. So he'd pushed her away, out of his arms, out of his life. Coldly, almost brutally telling her to go away, to grow up.

For the past nearly ten years they saw each other only at Colton family gatherings—which were only slightly less populated than some small countries. They acknowledged each other, but they'd never been alone together since that night.

They weren't alone now. Joe was standing on the

other side of the bed, tears streaming down his face as he held his daughter's limp hand.

"She's going to be fine, Joe," River assured him, wincing at the sight of Sophie's bruised and battered face, the bandages he could see peeking out above the slack neckline of the hospital gown. She looked as if she'd been dragged behind a runaway horse, her tender white skin scraped raw in spots, swollen and in livid shades of purple in others.

The largest bandage covered the left side of her face. There were more than one hundred stitches beneath that bandage. Her knee would heal. He'd make sure of that, even if he had to carry her on his back until the ligaments and tendons grew strong again. The scrapes and bruises, the scratches, would heal.

But her face? Sophie had never been vain, but she was young, only twenty-seven, and beautiful. How would she react to a scar on her face? A scar that reminded her, each and every time she looked in the mirror, of the terror she must have felt in that alley?

The mugger hadn't just hurt her physically. River feared that he might also have destroyed her confidence, badly scarred her in ways not so readily apparent. Robbed her of her freedom, her ability to walk down a street without fear.

River ran a hand through his shoulder-length black hair, rubbed at the back of his neck. His eyes sparkled with unshed tears that threatened to spill down over his lean, deeply tanned cheeks.

On the bed, Sophie stirred slightly, moaned, seemed to be trying to open her eyes.

"I…um…I'll get the nurse," River said quietly as

Sophie's eyes fluttered open for a second, then closed once more. "But I'll give you and Sophie a couple minutes alone together before I do."

He turned on his heels and left the room, his worn cowboy boots barely making any noise against the tile floor. The door closed behind him and he stopped in the hallway, one denim-clad shoulder leaning against the wall, his right fist dug deep in his jean pocket as he used his left to rhythmically beat the cowboy hat against his thigh.

River James looked like exactly who he was. A cowboy. A cowboy whose mother had been a full-blooded Native American, and whose father had been a white man. He had the thick black hair of his mother, the vivid green eyes of his father, and the disposition of a man most wouldn't lightly try to cross. Tall, whipcord lean, well muscled, hardened by years in the saddle as well as his unhappy life until the day Joe and Meredith Colton had taken him in, wised him up and given him a reason to believe he was somebody.

Until then, he'd been like a lone wolf. And once Sophie had gone out of his life, he'd reverted to that lone-wolf state. Complete unto himself. He didn't need Sophie, he didn't need anyone. At least that was what he'd been telling himself.

He'd been lying to himself.

It had been a long time since the thirty-one-year-old River James had felt helpless, defeated. It had not, however, been quite so long since he'd been angry. His temper had been his biggest problem when he'd come to Joe Colton's house as a teenager, and even if that anger had turned into something closer to pride, it was never far from the surface—not where Sophie Colton was concerned.

He'd been angry with her for pestering him. He'd been angry with her for growing up, for making him aware of her as more than his "sister." He'd been angry with her when he'd kissed her, when she'd tasted so good and he'd wanted her so much.

He'd been angry when she'd done the right thing and gone away, angry when she'd stayed away. Angry when she'd brought that idiot Chet Wallace to the ranch and announced that she was actually going to marry that grinning, three-piece suit—her engagement telling River that she didn't want someone like him, but wanted someone who was his complete opposite.

Now he was angry with her for lying in that hospital bed, looking so damn fragile, so damn beautiful, and for making him wake up, yet again, to the fact that he loved her.

Had always loved her. Would always love her.

Two

Joe Colton leaned over his daughter's bed and squeezed her hand. "Sophie? Sophie, honey? It's Dad."

Sophie stirred slightly on the bed, winced, then opened her eyes. "Daddy?" she asked, her voice weak.

Joe nodded, unable to speak. She hadn't called him Daddy in years. Now he was "Dad," sometimes, when she was being silly, "Senator." But she was still his baby girl, and as she looked up at him, as her bruised bottom lip began to tremble, he would have cut out his own heart if it could take away just a little of her pain.

"Oh, Daddy, it—it was horrible," Sophie told him, squeezing her eyes shut. "But I fought him, Daddy,

I fought him. Couldn't...Michael...couldn't let anything hurt you and Mommy again.''

"Hush, baby," Joe said, carefully stroking Sophie's hair. "Just rest, baby. All we want you to do is rest.''

Mary came into the room, and Joe stepped back from the bed to join River as the nurse took Sophie's vital signs, checked her IV.

"She's sleeping again?" River asked the senator.

"I think so," Joe said, nodding. "Look, River, it's been a long night, and I know you have to get back to the ranch. That new stallion's coming in today, right? So you just go, and I'll get a hotel room and stay until Sophie can come back to the ranch with us. Okay?''

A muscle ticked in River's cheek. He wasn't being dismissed. He knew that. Joe just wanted to be alone with his daughter. "What about Meredith? Do you think she'll want me to fly her here, to see Sophie, be with you?''

Joe Colton pressed his fingers against his eyes and shook his head. "I'll phone her later. Right now I just want to stay here.''

River nodded and patted Joe's back. "I'll call around, make a reservation for you, and then head back to the ranch. You'll phone later? Keep me— keep us informed?''

Joe didn't answer him. Mary brushed past them, leaving the room, and Joe headed toward the bed once more, dragging a utilitarian metal chair with him, then sat down beside Sophie, obviously dug in for the duration.

River left them alone and headed back down the hallway, toward the elevators. He was family, yes, and had been since his teenage years. He wasn't being dismissed, pushed away. But blood was blood, and Joe and Sophie were blood. River understood that, respected that.

The elevator doors opened as he approached, and Chet Wallace stepped out, looking as fresh and unwrinkled as if he'd just come out of the shower. His hair was combed, his face had been freshly shaved, his tie was snug against his throat. He could have been on his way to a morning meeting.

"Wallace," River bit out, taking hold of the man's elbow as Chet walked past him without so much as a nod. "Where've you been? Consulting with your tailor?"

"I beg your pardon," Chet answered, trying to shake off River's hand, without success. "Do I know— Oh, wait. You're one of the employees at Hacienda del Alegria, aren't you? Sophie's parents' ranch? I think I remember you now. Are the senator and his wife here already? I went back to my condo, caught some sleep, showered and changed."

"How nice for you," River said, finally letting go of Chet's elbow. "The senator is with Sophie now," he continued, motioning for Wallace to follow him into a small alcove set aside as a visitors' waiting room. "Let's talk."

"I'd rather speak with the senator," Chet said, but River's slitted-eye glare seemed to make him reconsider, and he followed River into the alcove. "Now, look—"

"No, Wallace, *you* look," River shot back, knowing he was going to have to perform a minor miracle if he expected to keep his temper in check. The man had gone home? Grabbed a few winks and taken a shower? No-good son of a bitch. "My name is James. River James, one of Joe and Meredith's foster children, not that you need to know any of that. What *I* need to know is why you let Sophie walk home alone last night. Or do the police have that wrong?"

Chet looked at River for a few moments, then shot his cuffs. He was a tall man, as tall as River, but that was where their similarities ended. Chet was sleek, pretty boy handsome, the kind of guy who wore designer sweats as he worked out at his designer gym. Shooting his cuffs, wordlessly pointing out that he was a successful man wearing a six-hundred-dollar suit, was an action meant to intimidate River.

Yeah, sure. River didn't think so. He just stood there, glaring at Chet Wallace, a tic working in his cheek, his hands itching to take the stylishly dressed man apart, piece by designer-label piece.

Chet broke eye contact first, his artificially tanned cheeks flushing slightly as he actually stepped back a pace, as if it had finally hit him that River James was a wild animal searching for prey, and that he was reacting pretty much like a deer caught out in the open.

In self-defense, Chet went on the attack. "Now look—James, is it? I already spoke with the police. Yes, Sophie and I had dinner together last night, and then she decided to walk home. Four blocks, James, that's all. As a matter of fact, I was just leaving the restaurant myself when I saw all the police cars and the ambulance. I went to check and found Sophie. I'm the one who identified her.''

"Well, bully for you. Why did she decide to walk home, Wallace?" River asked, putting his cowboy hat on, then looping his thumbs through his belt. "You two have a little spat? That is what you'd call it, right? A little spat?"

Chet's hand went to his Windsor knot, and he lifted his chin as he nervously shifted the tie from side to side. "We had a slight disagreement, yes," he conceded. "Not that it's any concern of yours."

"I don't care if you had the mother of all knock-down drag-outs, Wallace," River told him tightly. "That's none of my business. What I do care about is that you let her walk home alone."

Chet held up one hand. "Oh, wait a minute, fella. You're trying to say this is *my* fault? How does any of this become *my* fault? It was Sophie who went running off, you know. It was Sophie who— What? What's your problem?"

River had bent his head, rubbed his temples with the fingers of his right hand and laughed. He'd thought, really believed, he could get through this without losing his cool. But this Wallace was too thick for words, and River wasn't going to waste any more of his words on the jackass. He almost wanted to thank him for being so dense.

"My problem, Wallace?" River repeated, dropping his hand and looking at Sophie's fiancé. And then, before he could remember that he was, for the most part, a highly civilized individual, he planted his right fist square in Chet Wallace's face.

Chet went down on his backside, holding a hand to his bloody nose.

"Problem? I don't have a problem," River said, settling his worn cowboy hat lower over his flashing green eyes. "Not anymore."

Then he turned on his heels and headed for the elevator. He was not a happy man, definitely. But he was feeling somewhat better. Definitely.

For the next week, Joe Colton was never far from his daughter's bedside. His many businesses didn't suffer, because he'd been slowly withdrawing from those businesses, from his family, withdrawing from life itself. He'd allowed life to defeat him, again. Had it taken almost losing his daughter to wake him up, shake him up, force him to look at his life, possibly begin taking steps to fix it?

And when had it all begun to go so wrong?

Michael. Joe sighed, his heart aching as he remembered Sophie's words that first day, her garbled thoughts that, to anyone else, would have seemed as if she were talking crazy because of her concussion.

But Joe knew differently. He knew what his daughter had meant, and was devastated that, as she struggled with her attacker, her thoughts had been of Michael. Of Meredith and himself. Of the family, and of how the Colton family couldn't take another tragedy. Couldn't lose another child.

In a way, Michael had saved Sophie, and that was

how Joe was going to look at the thing. It was the only way possible to look at it.

Still, he had to look further than that, and he knew it. As he sat in the chair beside Sophie's hospital bed, holding her hand, watching her sleep, he had to acknowledge that Sophie had been slowly slipping away from him these past years. All his children had been slipping away, visiting the ranch less and less, avoiding the family that was no longer a family.

At least not the family it had been, the family he and Meredith had brought into the world, added to with adopted and foster children after Michael's death, family they'd formed into a solid, unbreakable, unshakable unit.

So when had it all begun to change? With Michael's death? Should he at least start there?

Probably.

Joe and Meredith had been raising five children. Rand, the oldest. The twins, Drake and Michael. Sophie and the baby, Amber. Life was good, better than good. Joe Colton was a rich, self-made man, with oil and gas interests, major investments in the communications industry. Meredith had even convinced him that it was time he gave something back, so that he'd run for the United States Senate and been elected to represent California.

Life was so good. So very good.

And then Michael and his twin had taken their bikes out for a ride, and Michael had been run down by a reckless driver. Dead, at the age of eleven, and while his father was away in Washington, instead of being home where he belonged. Home, keeping his children safe.

Joe pulled a handkerchief from his jacket pocket and wiped his forehead. His body was hot, his muscles tired, his brain stuffed with memory toppling over memory, few of those memories good.

Joe had resigned from the Senate, come home and made a jackass out of himself. He didn't see Meredith's grief. He didn't see Drake's special loss, the loss all his children had suffered. All he saw was his own pain, his own guilt. And when Meredith finally suggested they have another baby—not to replace Michael, surely, but because having another child to love might help them all heal—another bomb had dropped into Joe's shattered life.

He was sterile. How could that be? But it was true. He'd caught the mumps from a child at the nearby Hopechest Ranch, a home for orphaned children he and Meredith often visited, and now he was sterile. He could not give Meredith another child.

Was that when Meredith had begun to turn away from him?

No, that wasn't it, and Joe knew it. Meredith had stuck with him day and night, even when he was being a selfish, self-pitying jackass.

And it had been Meredith who had finally convinced him that there were many, many children who needed loving homes, many children they could help, who could help them, for Joe and Meredith still had so much love to give.

Joe smiled slightly as he remembered how Meredith had jumped in with both feet, taking on the most troubled children at the Hopechest Ranch, opening their house and her loving arms to Chance, to Tripp, to Rebecca, to Wyatt. To Blake, to River, and to Emily. To Joe Junior, the infant who had been literally left on their doorstep.

Emily. Joe's thoughts, which had begun to ease, now plunged him back into despair. Because the life he and Meredith had lost when Michael died, the one they'd rebuilt together—not a better life, surely, but a different one, a fulfilling one—had shattered again nine years ago, not six months after Joe Junior had come into their lives, on the day Meredith had driven the then eleven-year-old Emily into town for a visit with her natural grandmother.

Yes. That had been the day the light had forever gone out of Joe's life, out of the Colton family.

It was a small accident with the car, although there were never any small accidents. Each took its own toll. This particular one had taken Meredith from him, his beloved Meredith. Not in death, but in a head injury that had changed her in some way.

Emily had said her "good mommy" had been replaced by an "evil mommy." That was, of course, too simplistic, although even the doctors who had treated Meredith were at a loss as to why her personality had undergone such a dramatic change after the accident.

Change? No, that was too mundane a word to explain what had happened to Meredith. His sweet, loving wife, the concerned mother, had been taken from them, to be replaced by a woman who cared only for Joe Junior, a woman who ignored her other children,

a woman who positively despised and shunned Emily.
A woman who had turned hard, and selfish, and
grasping. A woman who had dared to present him
with her pregnancy a year after the accident and insist
he was the father.

They'd separated then, for long months, but Joe
had finally relented, let her come home, even claimed
the child, Teddy, as his own.

But nothing was the same. Nothing would ever be
the same again.

"Dad?"

Joe leaned closer to Sophie, who was looking up
at him with Meredith's beautiful brown eyes. "Yes,
baby?" Now that she was recovering, she didn't call
him Daddy anymore. But she was still his baby.

"Did Mom call you back yet? Is she coming?"

Joe felt a stab straight to his heart. "No, baby, your
mom couldn't be here. She's at home, taking care of
Joe Junior and Teddy."

"Oh," Sophie said, disappointment dimming her
eyes. "But she is coming soon, isn't she? It's been a
week, Dad."

"Shhh, baby, don't talk too much," Joe said, stroking Sophie's hair. "You need to rest now. You rest
and get strong, and soon we'll be able to go to the
ranch and see everybody. All right?"

"She's not coming, is she?" Sophie looked up at
her father, willing him to answer. "Is she, Dad?"

"You know how she doesn't like to leave
Teddy—"

Sophie held up a hand, wordlessly begging her father not to make excuses for her mother. "Teddy's

eight years old, Dad. Surely she could leave him for two or three days to visit me. There are plenty of people on the ranch who would take care of him. Oh, never mind. Why should I think things would be any different now than they have been for almost the last decade? You know, Dad, there are times when I feel this overwhelming urge to call my mother and ask for her help, because something's terribly wrong with my mother.''

Joe was rescued from having to find some way to respond to Sophie's heartbreaking remark by the entrance of Dr. Hardy, who had come to remove the stitches in Sophie's face.

''Good morning, Sophie, Senator,'' the cosmetic surgeon said, handsome and imposing in his green scrubs. ''Final unveiling today, Sophie. Are you ready?''

Sophie's hand tightened around Joe's. ''I guess so,'' she said quietly.

''Good,'' Dr. Hardy said, nodding as a nurse entered and handed him a paper package containing a pair of sterile gloves. ''Now remember, Sophie, this isn't the completed look. You're sort of a work in progress. You'll be swollen, bruised, and the cut is still going to look red, angry. That's to be expected. Later, in, oh, about six months, we'll go back to the operating room for a little of my magic. Isn't that right, Alice?'' he asked the nurse. ''Tell Sophie. I'm a magician.''

The nurse rolled her eyes, then grinned at the doctor, obviously the object of some substantial hero worship. ''I don't know about the magic part, Doctor, but I do know that Miss Colton has nothing to worry about. That scar is as good as gone."

"Thank you, Alice, and there'll be a little something extra in your paycheck this week," Dr. Hardy said, winking at Sophie, then advancing toward the bed even as Sophie began to cringe against the pillows. "No, no, Sophie. We're going to make this as quick and painless as possible, I promise. Alice is going to remove the bandages and then we'll get those stitches out of there before they start to do more harm than good. And then, young lady, you, your crutches and your leg brace get to go home—at least that's the word on the street. Okay? Is that a deal?"

"Dad?" Sophie said, squeezing Joe's hand until his circulation was all but cut off. "You'll get me a mirror. You promised."

Joe nodded, his throat clogged with tears, with fear for how the scar would look, how its appearance would impact his daughter. She'd only allowed Chet to visit her a single time, and had kept her head averted during the visit, so that she hadn't even asked him about the bandage over his nose. And then she'd made him promise not to try to see her again until she contacted him.

Joe wasn't sure if she was angry with her fiancé, if she blamed him for her attack or if she was afraid that her appearance had been ruined, so that Chet would be disgusted with her, repelled by her scar.

No matter what Sophie felt, however, Joe had already made up his mind that any man who would stay away from the bedside of his injured fiancée because she *told* him to…well, he wasn't the man for his Sophie!

Joe blinked, surprised to see that the bandage was already gone, and that Dr. Hardy was in the process of removing the stitches, his green-clad frame blocking Joe's view of his daughter's face.

And then it was done, and Sophie was nervously asking for the mirror.

"Maybe later, baby," Joe said, only to be cut off by Dr. Hardy, who took a mirror from Alice and handed it to Sophie.

"Just don't get used to how you look, Sophie, because that's going to change—not that it's looking so bad right now, in my opinion. You're young, your health is excellent, and I expect the final scar to be almost invisible."

Sophie held the mirror in front of her, slowly lifted her hand to tentatively touch the livid red wound that stretched from just below her ear, up and over her jawbone, then back down, so that it ran under her chin.

"He—he didn't make a very clean cut, did he?" she asked at last, putting down the mirror. "I could be marked with a big S, for Sophie. Or for Scarred," she ended, biting her bottom lip between her teeth.

Joe reached for her hand, but Dr. Hardy had already taken both of Sophie's hands in his. "Look at me, Sophie," he said, all traces of humor gone. "Look at me, sweetheart, and listen to me. It's a scar. That's all it is. And it will be gone soon, or as close to gone that you'll forget it's even there. But that scar, visible or not, isn't *you*. Do you understand that? If that's an

S on your jaw right now, it stands for Survivor. Don't forget that.''

Sophie nodded, and Dr. Hardy and his nurse left the room.

"Sophie? He's right, you know," Joe said. "You are a survivor. And you're going to be fine. Five more weeks at your apartment with the nurse I've hired, until the orthopods take that brace off your leg, and then you'll be with us, at the ranch. Six months from now, once Dr. Hardy is done with his magic, it will be as if this never happened.''

"But it did happen, Dad," Sophie told him, a huge tear slipping down her cheek. "Every night when I close my eyes I remember that it happened. Every day, now that the bandage is off, I won't be able to forget that it happened.''

She tugged her hand free of Joe's and pulled the large diamond ring from her third finger, left hand. "Here," she said, handing the ring to Joe. "Tell Chet I'll see him in six months, not before then.''

"Oh, honey, don't do this," Joe begged her, while inwardly he relaxed, with at least one problem being solved for him. "I'm sure Chet will be banging down the door to see you, to change your mind.''

"Like he's been banging down the door all week?" Sophie asked, her smile wry. "No, Dad. I just want to go home to my apartment, wait for this thing to come off my leg, and then come to the ranch. If you want me there?''

"If I— Ah, baby," Joe said, folding his daughter into his strong arms. "All I want out of life right now is to have you home with us again.''

Three

***

Home. It had never looked so good.

Sophie sat in the passenger seat as her father drove the car along the private roadway, past various ranch buildings, heading toward the huge, circular drive that fronted Hacienda del Alegria—the House of Joy.

She gave a small, lopsided smile as she remembered the day River had told her about another House of Joy, somewhere in Nevada, that had been a top-notch "pleasure palace" in its heyday, years earlier. Sophie had been highly affronted, saying that wasn't what her parents had in mind when they'd named the ranch, and then minutes later had retold the story to her oldest brother, Rand, giggling as he looked shocked that his little sister would even know about such things.

River had gotten into big trouble over that one—

which served him right, because Sophie had also been subjected to quite a lecture from Rand on what a lady isn't supposed to let anyone know she knows, even if she knows it.

Sophie held up a hand and squinted into the setting sun as the car entered the huge circular drive. Nothing had changed since her last visit. Nothing altered the physical beauty that was Hacienda del Alegria.

There was still the central area of the house, a two-story, sand-color adobe structure sporting California's version of a pillared porch, and a terra-cotta roof.

The sun still rose against the front windows, and set behind the house, over the wonderfully blue Pacific Ocean that lay below a series of cliffs.

Single-story wings wrapped back from either side of the house, affording every room a view of the ocean, of the marvelous gardens, of the courtyard, pool, and gardens that played such a large role in the everyday life of everyone who lived in the house.

And so many, many people had lived in Hacienda del Alegria over the years. Her parents occupied a large suite in the south wing, Sophie's and Amber's bedrooms were also located there, with the north wing housing their brothers and foster siblings.

A full house. A lovely house. Once a happy house.

But not anymore.

"Luckily you'll have no stairs to navigate," Joe Colton told his daughter as he stopped the car and turned off the ignition. "Even with the brace off, I think you're going to have to get used to being called Gimpy for a while, at least by your brothers. Just remember, Sophie, it's a measure of their affection.

Everyone's been worried sick about you. Boys just often don't know how to say what's really in their hearts."

Sophie smiled, shook her head at her father. "Senator, you know, you never cease to amaze me. How can you still be giving us all lessons? Did it ever occur to you that we might be grown up now?"

"Never. Not in my wildest dreams," Joe answered, reaching over to flick a fingertip against Sophie's nose. She flinched at the near contact and turned her head, raising a hand to the scar on her left cheek.

"Baby—"

"Not now, Dad," Sophie said tightly. She'd been nervous ever since they'd gotten within twenty miles of the ranch. Nervous about her welcome, who would be there to welcome her home, what they'd think when they saw her. "Let's just get inside, okay?"

Leaving the baggage in the trunk, Joe quickly came around and opened the car door for Sophie, then walked with her to the front door that stood open in welcome. Their housekeeper, Inez Ramirez, waited there, a broad smile on her wide, pleasant face. "Welcome home, Miss Sophie," Inez said, holding out her arms, and Sophie gratefully walked into them, allowing the hug, needing the hug.

Then it was time to pass into the large great room that made up the nerve center of the house, a huge room furnished well, but casually.

The empty room.

"Dad?" Sophie asked, turning to her father, who then pointed toward the wall of glass doors leading out to the courtyard. Following his gesture, Sophie could see Meredith Colton lounging on a chaise beside the pool, clad in a bra-like swim top and a long, filmy, patterned skirt, dark glasses shading her eyes.

"I'll go get her," Joe offered, but Sophie shook her head and started for the doors. "Sophie, she couldn't know the exact time we'd arrive," he called after her, then swore under his breath and quickly turned his back on a scene he didn't have the strength to witness.

Sophie limped out onto the patio, slowly made her way down the steps and past the fountain. The beauty of the courtyard was lost to her, its sights, its sounds, its glorious smells. All she could see was her mother, the woman who had spoken to her on the telephone only a single time in the past six weeks, the woman who hadn't had the time or the inclination to visit her in San Francisco.

Sophie stood beside the chaise and looked down at the woman who had taught her how to tie her shoes, who had giggled with her when Sophie had tried on her very first training bra, who had put up her hair for her the night of the senior prom. The woman who had kissed her cuts and scrapes, hand sewn her Princess Leia Halloween costume, held her when she cried because River James was just the most awful, miserable, nasty boy in the whole entire world.

Who are you? Sophie asked silently, gazing down at the sunscreen-slick woman with the bloodred fingernails, the perfectly coiffed golden-brown hair, the too-youthful swimsuit…the pitcher of martinis on the table beside her. *Who are you? Because you aren't my mother anymore. You can't be my mother.*

"Hello, Mother," Sophie said at last, when Meredith Colton didn't respond to her presence. "I'm home."

Meredith raised a hand, removed her sunglasses, then slid her long legs to one side and stood, looking at Sophie with Sophie's own huge brown eyes. "Well, so you are," she said, motioning toward the metal cane in Sophie's left hand. "Is *that* going to be around for much longer? I mean, really, it's so... medical. Couldn't you find something nicer?"

"It's good to see you, too, Mom," Sophie said, giving in to her fatigue and sitting down on the matching chaise. She kept her head down, so that the curtain of her hair slid forward, covering her cheek.

"Don't be snide, Sophie," Meredith told her, sitting down again herself and taking hold of her martini glass. "Or hasn't it yet occurred to you that you're twenty-seven years old? Old enough to move to San Francisco. Old enough to be out on your own, just as you wanted to be. You wanted to be independent, and I let you be independent. But, obviously, for all that independence, you're still not so grown up that you couldn't insist that your doting daddy jump up and run when you wanted him."

Shock made Sophie lift her head, and she watched in horror as Meredith's eyes widened at the sight of the scar. She raised a hand to her jaw, but it was too late, because her mother had seen everything there was to see.

Meredith's upper lip curled in distaste. "Not bad? That's what your father said. The scar wasn't *bad*. Doesn't the man have eyes in his head? Oh, you poor thing. How are you going to manage, being so horribly disfigured like that? And your father says you sent Chet away? That wasn't smart, Sophie. How do you expect to get another man with that ruined face? I really think you should— Where are you going? Is this how you were raised? How dare you walk away while I'm speaking to you. I'm your *mother!*''

But Sophie had gotten to her feet as quickly as she could and was already hobbling back toward the house, wondering what on earth had possessed her to come home. Whoever had said it had been right: You can't go home again.

At least not to Hacienda del Alegria. The House of Joy?

No, not anymore.

River walked back to the stables after watching Joe's car drive past, seeing Sophie's form in the passenger seat.

So. She was home. Healing, but not quite mended. And without a diamond on her third finger, left hand.

Not that he was going to do anything about that, *could* do anything about that.

Besides, it might only be temporary, some sort of emotional fallout from the mugging. Joe had told him how sensitive Sophie was about the cut on her face, how she refused to see that the scar was fading every day, growing less obvious to everyone but her.

If nobody mentioned the scar, made a big deal about it, Sophie would probably soon be able to deal with the thing, put it behind her, look forward to the surgery that would finish the job the doctor had begun and her healthy body had taken from there. After all, her knee was already so good that the J-brace and crutches were gone.

She'd been in physical therapy in San Francisco almost from the beginning, and now that she would soon be putting aside her cane, the therapy could begin in earnest, building up muscles grown weak from disuse.

Sophie was fine. Fine. And she was going to be even better.

River told himself that every night. She was healing. She was back with her family, who would do everything in their power to help her heal. She'd soon be his own laughing, happy, optimistic Sophie again.

Please, God.

River busied himself in the tack room, making up excuse after excuse not to leave the stables, not to head up to the house. See Sophie.

She'd be too busy for him anyway, with everyone else crowding around, hugging her, kissing her, welcoming her back. Why, he might even take dinner out here with the boys rather than go up to the house for the evening meal. That wasn't so unusual; he did it all the time.

"Coward," he muttered under his breath as he hung up the bridle he'd just inspected. "What do you think she's going to do, buddy? Bite your head off?" He lowered his head and sighed. "Ignore you?"

Okay, so now he was finally getting down to it. She might ignore him—or worse, treat him the same as she did her brothers and sister, her foster siblings. Happy to see him, polite, even loving. But not special.

Not the way they'd been, years ago.

He wouldn't have made it without Sophie, wouldn't have survived. He knew it, even if she didn't.

River had come to the ranch a rebellious teenager—alternately hotheaded and morose, a teeming mass of hate and anger and, often, despair. He lashed out at anyone who came near him, tried to help him, although he didn't realize until many years later that he kept people at arm's length because he was too afraid to let anyone into his world, for fear they'd leave him.

He'd been born to a white rancher and a Native American mother whom his father had married only because he'd been careless and put a child in her belly, River. His father resented his Native American wife, and Rafe, her son from a previous marriage, but that didn't mean he kept his hands off her.

River's earliest memories were of his mother's love and his father's undisguised disgust.

And then his mother left him, died in childbirth when he was only six. His new sister, Cheyenne, was taken in by her maternal grandmother, to be raised on reservation land. Rafe, River's protector, also stayed on the reservation, because their father didn't want him, couldn't control him. But not River. Oh, no, he wanted River. He was six years old now. Old enough to "help" eke out a poor living on that small, decrepit excuse for a ranch. Old enough to do a "man's" work. Rafe, on the other hand, was old enough to talk back, and so he was left behind, considered worthless, too much the savage for his stepfather to have to face every day.

All the love went out of River's life when his mother died, when his sister and brother had been taken away. His own life was reduced to caring for and avoiding the slaps from a rotten drunk.

School was a place River went when his father was passed out drunk on the couch and couldn't stop him, saddle him with another chore. It was at school, when River was nine, that one of his teachers had seen the bruises.

Now his father was gone, left at the ranch while River was removed from his not-so-tender care and placed at the Hopechest Ranch, a haven for children from "troubled homes."

He'd hated it there. Hated the kindness, the caring, the promise that he was safe now, had nothing to worry about anymore. What did those do-gooders know? He was *alone,* that was what he was. His mother gone, his Native American family unwilling or unable to take him, his father a brutal drunk who could show up at any moment, drag him back to the ranch.

River found some solace with the horses at Hope-chest Ranch, a project initiated by Joe Colton, a charitable contribution he believed would help the children who cared for the horses, learned responsibility through that care, and in return were given something to love.

That was how it began. River James, half-breed and teenage menace, and Joe Colton, rich man, senator, and a man stubborn enough to ignore River's animosity, his rebuffs, and finally take the troubled teen into his own home.

Joe and Meredith tried their best, they really did. So did the other Coltons. But River held out, held himself aloof from them all, ignoring their kindness while spending his days cutting school and hanging out at the stables. Hacienda del Alegria wasn't exactly a working ranch, but Joe Colton did raise horses, and that was enough for River.

Except he couldn't shrug off Sophie Colton, because the girl simply refused to go away, to leave him alone. God, how he'd tried to send her away. Called her names, ignored her, let her know her company wasn't welcome.

For all the good it did him.

Just entering her teens, Sophie had been skinny as a Popsicle stick and just as physically two-dimensional. Bright silver braces on her teeth. Silly pigtails in her hair. With a curiosity that drove him nearly insane as she tagged after him asking "Why?" and "How'dya do that?" and "Can I ride him next, huh, huh, can I?"

He longed to strangle her, because she wouldn't give up. Her tenacity infuriated him, right up until the moment he realized that Sophie Colton was special. All the Coltons were special, but Sophie was extraordinary. She had a heart so big it included the whole world, even him. She wore him down, wormed her way through his defenses, and the two of them became friends, more than friends. Inseparable.

And then she had to ruin it all and grow up, start seeing him as her boyfriend, her first love. God, that had been hard. Especially since River *felt* like her boyfriend, wanted to be the one who awakened Sophie to love, then held her in his arms forever.

He'd been a fool to agree to escort her to her senior prom, more of a fool to kiss her.

And then she'd gone away, and his last sight of her had been the tears in those huge brown eyes when he'd told her to go away, to grow up, to leave him alone.

He should have left then, left the ranch, left the Coltons. He was old enough to be on his own, legally free to leave. But then there was that mess with Meredith, the marital separation that had so unsettled everyone, and Joe's unhappiness over these past nine years.

How could River leave the man who had given him so much? Even as word of River's expertise with horses traveled far enough to have ranchers from Colorado to Texas making him offers, River had stayed with Joe and built up the Colton stud.

He had stayed with Joe and waited for Sophie to come home, knowing she never would. Not with her successful career in San Francisco. Not with that damned ring on her finger. And most especially not to revisit the strained unhappiness that hung over the ranch.

"River? You back there?"

River walked out of the tack room, toward Joe Colton, who was standing in the stables, looking lost and defeated. "Senator? Is everything all right? I saw you drive up a while ago with Sophie."

River retrieved two soda cans from a small refrigerator and handed one to Joe, motioning for them to step outside, sit down on the bench against the wall, just to the left of the huge doors. ''Joe? Everything *is* all right, isn't it? I mean, you told me she was fine—''

Joe gave a slight wave of his hand. ''No, no, it's nothing like that. Sophie's doctors are over the moon with her progress, just as I told you. All of them. And they're satisfied that you'll make sure she gets to physical therapy in Prosperino three times a week. So, no, nothing's wrong there. It's just…it's just…''

''Meredith?'' River asked, his jaw tight. ''Tell me. What did she do?''

Joe, unable to sit still, got up and began to pace. ''It's more like what she didn't do. She does nothing, and it hurts Sophie. Then she finally does do something, and it hurts Sophie. The poor kid's in her room, crying her eyes out.''

''Sophie's crying? Why?'' River crushed the soda can, its contents spilling over his fingers, so that he tossed it into the garbage container beside the bench.

Joe sat down once more, his shoulders slumped, his hands locked together between his spread knees. ''Meredith didn't even watch for us, or come into the house when Inez told her we'd arrived. Inez took me to one side and told me she'd let Meredith know we'd arrived. But Meredith just stayed out at the pool, sunning herself, and then let Sophie know that her cane was ugly, her scar even more ugly. She told her…she told her she shouldn't have tossed Chet over because now she'll never get a man, not with that scar.''

River muttered a few choice words under his

breath, then sighed. That was Meredith. Always saying the wrong thing, never concerned for anyone except herself, and Joe Junior, and Teddy. Nobody else mattered to her anymore. She only seemed to use the other members of the Colton family to sharpen her claws on. ''Now what?''

Joe shrugged. ''I don't know, son. Sophie was already pretty shaky about that scar, but I figured she'd get over it now that she's here, with us. I never expected Meredith to— Aw, hell, River. What happened? What in hell happened to us?''

Four

Sophie had fled Meredith Colton's presence and run to her room—hobbled to her old bedroom—and thrown herself on her bed to cry. It had been a veritable storm of weeping, as she'd cried with huge gulping sobs, the sort she hadn't cried since her teenage years.

Since the night River had rejected her.

She'd come apart after Meredith's cold, cutting comments that had sliced at her, injuring her as much as the knife had done, possibly more. There was no pretty way to say it, no rationalization that could explain how thoroughly Sophie fell apart, how completely she finally gave in, gave herself up to her grief as everything that was wrong in her life came together at once, threatening to destroy her.

Sophie had held it together, held everything in,

since the first days after the mugging, once the pain-killers had been stopped and she had more control over her thoughts, her reactions. She couldn't let her father see how frightened she was, how defeated she felt. How violated. How used.

Because she'd known how nearly homicidal Joe had been, sitting beside her hospital bed as the police asked her for details of the attack, how impotent he still felt that he couldn't protect his child, keep her from all harm. He had stayed with her for two weeks, the first spent in the hospital, the second as she got settled back into her apartment, hovering over her, fussing over her, worrying about her, playing mother and father to her in his wife's absence.

She'd held back her tears as she slowly realized that Chet had taken her at her word. He didn't phone. He didn't come pounding on her door, demanding to see her. Yes, he had sent a note stuffed inside a soppy Get Well card, telling her that he loved her and he'd wait for her to "come to her senses."

That had hurt. Come to her senses? Is that what he thought? That she'd lost her senses? Didn't he understand? Didn't anyone understand?

She'd lost a lot more than her "senses."

When her dad had come into the room and gathered her into his arms, Sophie had told him what Meredith had said. She shouldn't have done that, really, she shouldn't have. But the loss she felt was so great, the hurt so overwhelming, that she hadn't been able to keep the truth from her father—the truth that her mother, her own mother, now considered her disfigured and a total loss.

"She's sick, baby," Joe had said to her, his words sounding sad and tired and eerily hollow. "Ever since the accident. Something happened. Something changed her. You just have to remember how she was, baby. We all have to remember that, remember how she once loved us."

That was when Sophie had gotten herself back under control. She couldn't bear to hear the defeat in her father's voice, the deep sadness that had to have been slowly destroying him these past nine years.

Sophie had hugged him, kissed him and promised to remember, to hold on to the memories of the good days. She listened as he discussed the physical therapy she'd begin in Prosperino in a few days, the surgery she'd have in less than five months, to minimize her scar.

She'd agreed with him on everything, assured him she was all right, and watched after him as he left her room, his large frame stooped, his feet dragging.

Her impulsively formed plan to leave the ranch the next morning embarrassed her as she watched her father. How could she leave him? How could she have stayed away so long? *Why* had she stayed away so long? Because of Meredith? Perhaps.

But there was another reason, and Sophie knew it.

She watched now as that reason walked toward her through the soft patches of misty yellow drifting down from the vapor lights placed around the stables.

He walked with his head down, his face hidden by that ever-present dusty tan cowboy hat that seemed so much a part of him. He had his hands stuffed deep in his jean pockets and kicked a stone along the drive with the tip of his worn cowboy boots. The lone wolf, prowling his nocturnal territory.

Sophie's stomach muscles clenched as she watched him approach, drank in the sight of him. Long and lean, his shoulders broad, his waist and hips narrow, his straight legs wrapped tight in faded jeans. He moved gracefully, unaware of his natural grace.

When she had been a kid, she'd marveled at his shoulder-length hair, black as night, straight as sticks, and the perfect frame for his tanned, brooding face, his sparkling green eyes, the intriguing slashes that appeared in his cheeks at his rare smiles.

River had figured in all her dreams for just about as long as she could remember having dreams. The barely tamed rebel, the exotic creature with a Native American mother and a father who had tried, and failed, to destroy him. The misfit. The one person on the ranch who didn't immediately love her, think she was wonderful, do anything and everything to please her.

A creature of light, Sophie had been drawn to his darkness, his secrets. He spoke to the horses, whispered to them, and they listened. He stood toe to toe with her father, the only person Sophie had ever seen do that, and never backed down. Never backed down from anyone, from anything.

He was wild, and wonderful, and Sophie would have done anything for his smile, a single word of praise, to have him notice her, talk to her, let her into at least a small slice of his life.

No, Sophie knew that she hadn't stayed away from the ranch because her family had changed while she was gone at college. She'd gone, and stayed away, because River hadn't wanted her.

Everything she had done since the night he had kissed her then pushed her away, told her to go away, had been to hurt River. Her choice of career. Her engagement to Chet Wallace, who was as different from River James as a pin-striped three-piece suit was from a battered cowboy hat pushed down low over all-seeing green eyes.

River had always been strong, definitely stronger than her. Because he had stayed, he had taken the good with the bad, raised himself above a truly tragic childhood. Stayed to give back for all he'd been given.

She watched as he lifted his head and saw her sitting on the bench. His step faltered for a moment, and then he walked toward her with his lazy, rolling gait, sat down beside her in the space she'd left for him— on her right, so that he couldn't see her scar. Not that he could see much more than form and shadow in this spot just out of the reach of any of the vapor lights, but she just felt more comfortable with her left cheek hidden.

"Evening, Sophie. Welcome home," he said, the sound of his voice soft, smooth. It was a voice that could soothe a frightened horse, spin a young girl wonderful stories of Native American life as it had been before the white man came. A voice that could whisper, "I want you. God, Sophie, how I want you."

Sophie just nodded, her tongue cleaving to the roof of her suddenly dry mouth. He smelled of soap and shaving cream and something else, something undefinable, but definitely male. All male, all man.

"They were waiting for you up at the house," he said, leaning back against the side of the stables, his long legs stretched out in front of him, his head still bent forward, so that he didn't bang the rim of his hat against the wall. "Dinner's up."

"I know, Riv," she said, wondering if he could condense his sentences anymore, make them shorter, more clipped. It was as if he didn't want to talk to her at all. "I asked Inez to save me something in the refrigerator, in case I get hungry later. Riv, why did you tell me to leave?"

The moment the words were out of her mouth, she gasped and clapped a hand over her mouth. Had she gone mad? How could she have asked that?

He didn't react, didn't flinch. It was if he'd been expecting the question, maybe waiting for it. Waiting ten years for her to ask.

"It was time for you to go," he said, taking off his hat and placing it beside him on the bench. "Time for you to grow up, see the world, find out who Sophie Colton was." He turned toward her and tipped his head as he looked at her in the darkness. "Did you find her, Sophie? Did you like her?"

"I thought I did," she answered truthfully. "As long as I hated you, I liked myself."

River chuckled low in his throat. "That's my Sophie. Give her a good mad, and she can bring the world to its knees."

She smiled, in spite of herself. "You remember

that? You remember how I wanted to conquer the
world?"

"*Rule* the world, I think it was, actually," River
corrected her. "Right after you flew to Mars, cured
cancer and invented a pimple cream that really
worked—which would have been just before you won
the Pulitzer Prize. Yes, I remember. You had big-time
dreams, Sophie. Dreams that were a lot bigger than
this ranch."

"I was a kid, Riv," she shot back angrily. "What
the hell did I know about life?"

"Well, Sophie, that's just it. You didn't know
about life, did you? But you deserved a chance to find
out what was out there."

Sophie sniffed, shook her head. "What's out there,
Riv, is doing homey, tearjerker ads for health insur-
ance companies who withhold treatment to their cus-
tomers, writing jingles for pimple creams that *don't*
work…and a world that's a lot bigger, and stronger,
and meaner than I ever could have imagined." Her
voice broke slightly. "It knocked me down, Riv. The
world out there knocked me down."

"And so now you're home again. Damn, Sophie.
How do you sit there looking so comfortable, with
your tail tucked between your legs like that?"

She turned sideways on the bench and glared at
him. "You son of a— Damn it, Riv, shut up!" How
did he do it? How could he make her so mad?

He reached up and scratched at a spot just below
his left ear. "Hasn't worked any miracles for you yet,
has it, Soph? Coming home, that is. Joe told me about
Meredith's version of welcoming the prodigal back

into the fold this afternoon. Nice. Very nice. Very Meredith.''

''I'm not going to let her get to me,'' Sophie declared, trying to believe what she said, trying to tell herself that her mother's words hadn't hurt, didn't still hurt. ''She's sick. Dad says so. The car accident did something—she banged her head, jiggled her brains, shook up her personality. Or maybe it's...well, maybe it's the changes. Some women have real problems as they go through menopause.''

''Wrote up a hormone replacement ad for that company of yours, did you?'' River said, his even white teeth visible in the soft glow of light as he grinned at her. ''Wouldn't it be great if we could all talk in advertising slogans and actually believe all the promises? A thirty-second fix for everything from bad hair days to world peace, if only you used the right product, picked the right party, whatever. Do you do political ads, Sophie? I'll bet you do. Making silk purses out of sows' ears, and then ramming it all down the public's throat. Very commendable.''

Sophie clenched her hands into fists. ''If you're all done making fun of what I chose to do with my career...?''

''All done? Nope. I've got a few more stored away somewhere, but I guess I'll leave them there for now. But admit it, Sophie, I got your mind off that cheek you were keeping turned away from me until a few moments ago.''

She quickly lifted a hand to her cheek, turned her head. ''You never did play fair, did you, Riv?'' she asked, staring out into the night, blinking back tears.

"I—I didn't know you were so disappointed in the career I chose."

"You were going to do the internship at Joe's place in Texas, then major in Communications at college. Graduate, work at one of the television stations, or do investigative reporting for one of the Colton family newspapers. Be like your dad, one of the few men who have used public office, public responsibility, to really *help* people. Next thing I heard, you were making up slogans for tartar-reducing toothpaste, earning the big bucks, but selling out all your dreams. Hey, now *that's* really making a contribution, isn't it?"

"You don't understand," Sophie told him, once more forgetting about her scar, forgetting to hide that scar from River. "Those were *dreams,* Riv. Young girl dreams."

"So you really enjoy your work?"

"Of course I enjoy my work!" Sophie exploded, grabbing at her cane and rising to her feet. "I *love* what I do!"

"Funny. That's not what Rand told me."

Sophie sat down again. "Rand? I—I don't know what you mean."

"Really? You know, Sophie, you didn't use to lie to me."

She bit her bottom lip for a moment, then asked, "What did Rand say?"

"He said that you contacted him just after you and Wallace got engaged, because Wallace wanted the two of you to leave the advertising agency and set up one of your own. He said that you sounded less than enthused, partly because Wallace was talking his expertise and your capital, but also partly because you'd been thinking about getting out of the business.''

''And coming back here to write a book,'' Sophie ended for him, wincing as this very private dream seemed now to be everybody's business.

''Really? Write a book? Actually, Rand didn't say anything about that.''

''He shouldn't have said *anything*,'' Sophie blustered, to cover her embarrassment. ''I spoke to him as a lawyer, not my brother.''

''And Rand talked to me because he knows I care about you,'' River replied in that low, smooth voice that might have the power to soothe savage beasts, but only prodded Sophie into another white-hot streak of anger.

''*Care* about me? Oh, cut me a break, Riv,'' she said bitterly. ''If you'd truly cared about me, you'd never have let me— Oh damn!''

''Back to square one, aren't we?'' River asked her, reaching out, stroking her arm.

''Yeah, I suppose so,'' Sophie agreed. ''I left because you pushed me away, and now I'm back and the first thing I do is come chasing after you. Ten years, Riv, and it looks like I haven't learned a damn thing.''

River was silent for a long time, and Sophie began to relax, fall back into the sort of comfortable silences they used to share, times when it was enough to be with him, sitting under a starry sky, sharing his world.

''Meredith's full of crap, you know,'' he said at last, startling her. ''You're a beautiful woman. Even with both your eyes blackened, and bandages, and scrapes and bruises all over your face, you're the most beautiful woman I've ever known.''

Sophie closed her eyes, digested his words. "You were there? You saw me?"

"I flew the senator to San Francisco within an hour of getting the news about the mugging. So, yes, I saw you. I saw you, and then I broke pretty boy Wallace's nose for him because he let you walk home alone. Didn't he tell you?"

"I—I didn't know," Sophie said, remembering Chet's visit, vaguely remembering a bandage on his nose. She'd been so worried about her own appearance, and so angry with him, that she'd never really looked at him, never seen more of him than his carefully ironed shirt, his perfectly arranged necktie. "You punched him? You really *punched* him?"

"Real mature, wasn't I?" River said, shaking his head. "I guess I just needed to punch something— and lover-boy accommodated me."

"It wasn't Chet's fault," Sophie said, for the first time wondering if perhaps it was, if perhaps, just perhaps, that was why she didn't want to see him…and why he hadn't made any attempts to see her. "I'm the one that left the restaurant."

"And he's the one who let you leave," River responded without missing a beat.

"Yes, he was. And he wasn't the first man to let me leave, was he? I don't want to talk about this," Sophie said, rubbing her arms, as either the evening had turned colder, or her thoughts were sending a chill into her body. "I don't want to talk about any of this. I just want to *forget* it."

"Fine," River agreed, positioning his hat back on his head, standing up, holding out his hand to her. "Let's walk. We can talk about this book you want to write."

"Maybe some other time," Sophie told him, although she did put her hand in his and allow him to help her to her feet. "It's still just an idea, Riv, and I'd rather keep it to myself for a while longer."

"You used to tell me everything, including a bunch of stuff that, trust me, no teenage boy wanted to hear. Do you remember how you were so gung-ho to show me your first push-up bra? I damn near had to climb a tree to get away from that one."

Sophie ducked her head, grinned. "I was a real pain, wasn't I? Well, I promise not to be your resident pest anymore, okay?"

He turned to her and picked up her chin with his crooked index finger. "Oh, I don't know. I think I'd miss my resident pest. I think I have missed her, quite a lot. My pretty little pest, all grown up into a beautiful woman."

Sophie turned her head, so that he couldn't see her scar, then pulled away from him. "Don't do that, Riv," she told him, all but begged him. "Don't lie to me. I could always count on you never to lie to me."

River took hold of her shoulders and forced her to look at him. "What in hell are you talking about?"

"What am I— Oh, for God's sake, Riv! My *face!* I'm not the person you knew. The pest, the hero-worshipper, the idiot teenager who thought the sun rose and set on you. I'm not the career woman, I'm not Meredith's cherished child. I'm not anyone I know or recognize anymore. I'm scared of my own shadow, and everything I'd ever hoped or believed died in that damn alley. And I most certainly am *not* beautiful.''

''Ah, Sophie,'' River said, pulling her into his arms, even as she struggled to be free of him. ''Don't let the world win, sweetheart. You can't let the bad guys win.''

''Meredith? May I come in?''

Joe Colton stood just inside the door to his wife's bedroom, still able to be shocked by the overblown femininity of its furnishings, the lavish white Restoration French furniture and elaborate decorations that Meredith would once have called silly, and definitely shunned.

Then again, she had always slept with him, sharing his bed as she shared his life. Once, this bedroom had been done up in the Mission style, with hand loomed Native American rugs scattered on the hardwood floors. They'd furnished the room together, choosing each piece, surrounding themselves with memories of trips they'd taken, sights they'd seen, moments they'd shared.

Now Joe slept in a room down the hall, and asked permission to enter his wife's bedroom.

''Joe! How wonderful!'' Meredith exclaimed, walking toward him, her long-legged, still slim body barely covered by a white silk dressing gown. ''I've just been thinking about you.''

That could be good or bad, Joe knew, trying not to wince. Mostly it could be bad. ''Really, Meredith?''

"Yes, Joe, really," she snapped back at him, then smiled as she very noticeably tried to control her temper. "I've been thinking, to be precise, about your birthday party. The plans are coming along nicely. Your sixtieth will be quite a memorable event."

"They've all been memorable, Meredith," he reminded her. "We always have a party—"

"I do not consider throwing a pig on a fire and standing around eating from paper plates a *party*, Joe," Meredith told him, rolling her eyes. "This will be a *real* party. Senator Joe Colton's sixtieth birthday party."

She turned back to the small marble-topped secretary and picked up several sheets of monogrammed paper. "Look who's coming—members of congress, past and present, the governor of California, of course. Business leaders, the cream of the social crop, celebrities. Black tie, Joe, definitely. I have my eye on this Versace gown, and there's this new thing Frank has been dying to have me try with my hair—"

"Are you nuts?" Joe said before he could leash his tongue.

Meredith's brown eyes widened as her full mouth drew into a thin line. "Don't you say that, Joe Colton. Don't you *ever* say that," she told him through clenched teeth. "I am the mother of your children, remember?"

"You're the mother of children, yes," Joe said, pain slicing through him at the thought of Teddy, whom the woman had been vicious enough to name after Joe's father, and a man Joe would rather forget had ever existed. "Not all of them mine."

Meredith threw up her arms and sat down on the bench of her dressing table. "Here we go again, don't we? One small mistake, and I'm forever cursed. And none of it was your fault? You haven't touched me since the—"

"Do you want me to touch you, Meredith?" Joe asked, hating himself for still loving this woman, and yet thankful he could still remember the happy years, if only vaguely, as those memories were so encumbered by the baggage of the past decade.

"Joe Junior made this for me," Meredith said, changing the subject as she picked up a small blue misshapen clay vase painted with yellow daisies. "Isn't it sweet? Not that I'll keep it in here, of course."

Joe stabbed his fingers through his graying hair. "Yeah, it's great, Meredith. Really nice. Look, about this party—"

Meredith put down the vase, patted it, then turned to Joe once more. "You're going to love it, Joe. Our media companies will cover it, naturally, but there will be other press as well. I want everything to be perfect—even if that means having to put up with that awful old Sybil flying in from Paris. Can't stand her, but saying that guests have traveled from as far as Paris—well, it doesn't hurt."

"You've got your heart set on this, don't you, Meredith?" Joe asked, wondering when he'd gotten so tired that he couldn't even say no to his wife and have any chance of having her at least agree to listen to his protests.

"We're going to have a party, Joe," Meredith said,

her eyes flashing, her tone steely. "We'll have all the little chicks gathered to celebrate your birthday. A very special birthday, I promise you that." She stood up, walked over to wrap her arms around his shoulders. "I've got such plans, Joe. You wouldn't believe the plans I have."

He felt cold, not warmed by her closeness. As she lifted her face for his kiss, he pecked at her cheek, then removed her arms from his shoulders. "It's late," he said, moving away from her. "But I did want to talk to you about Sophie."

"Sophie? What about her? Poor little thing."

Joe's jaw tightened. "Sophie is *not* a poor little thing. She's your daughter, Meredith. How dare you tell her she's ruined."

Once more Meredith rolled her eyes. "And I'm telling her something her own mirror hasn't told her? I don't think so. And now I have to explain to Joe Junior and Teddy why she looks the way she does without frightening them. Did you think of that? Did you think of how upset my boys will be? Go away, Joe. I'm tired and I want to go to bed."

"Just stay away from her, okay? If you can't be supportive, stay away from her."

Meredith waved a hand at him as she walked toward her dressing room, obviously having dismissed him, and Joe left the room where his children had been conceived, where he had loved, and laughed, and once believed himself the happiest, luckiest man in the world.

He could divorce her, had thought about divorcing her when she had presented him with her pregnancy, but that wasn't the answer. She was Meredith, she was the woman he loved—had loved, still loved. And she was sick, ill. Mentally unstable, and unwilling to seek help. Could he force the issue? Have her committed, treated?

Joe winced, shook his head. No. No, he couldn't think about that, wouldn't think about that. Because she'd get better. Sophie was home, and that would help her. And they'd have the party, and she'd get all caught up in the plans, and she'd be happy.

And if it doesn't work? a voice in his head asked. If the party doesn't change things, if nothing changes things? What if she gets worse? What will you do then? How long are you going to wait before you do something?

"I'll do what I have to do," he said out loud, hearing the quaver in his own voice. "But, please God, not yet. This is my wife. My wife. I can't give up hope yet. I just can't."

Five

River didn't know where to put his hands. He held Sophie, let her cry. Patted her shoulder, rubbed her back.

And wanted so much more.

Her cane had dropped to the ground earlier, and she leaned heavily against him, her sobs slowly reduced to sniffles as he murmured some undoubtedly ridiculous, banal words of comfort that she didn't hear and he would probably hate himself for in the morning.

When was the last time she'd cried in his arms? Well, that was easy, because Sophie rarely cried, had always been the bravest person in the world, with her jutted-out chin, shining eyes, and a firm resolve not to let the world know when she was hurting.

He knew. The last time, the only time, had been the night of that damn silly senior prom.

He hadn't gone to his own—what would have been the point? He hadn't interacted in high school, hadn't given much of a damn, and would have skipped his own graduation if Joe and Meredith hadn't told him how sad they'd be to miss this great milestone in their foster son's life.

So he'd agreed to take Sophie to the dance. He'd dressed himself up in a monkey suit, clubbed his hair at his nape with a black ribbon, and even bought her an orchid corsage. Hating every moment of it.

Hating it, that was, until he'd watched Sophie come into the great room, her light-brown hair done in this fancy upsweep, her creamy shoulders bare above a simple white full-length sheath that clung to parts of her he'd been trying hard to forget existed.

"I know you'll take care of her, son," Joe had said as they'd passed into the night, on their way to a Prosperino hotel that boasted a ballroom. It had been a request. It had been an order.

And it had been a promise, a promise River had been doomed to break.

Sophie had set him up for a fall. With her hair, those maddening tendrils that so artfully curled against her slim neck. With her gown, that skimmed the soft swell of her breasts. With her perfume, a clean, wildflower scent that raised instincts in him that had been far from protective.

With her smile. With her arms around him, the top of her head against his chin as they danced. With her huge eyes, that looked up at him so trustingly, so eagerly.

He'd kissed her. How could he not kiss her? How could he let her leave in the morning, off to her internship, then straight to college, without holding her at least once, kissing her at least once?

But then she'd cried, begged him to tell her not to go. Begged him to tell her he loved her, as she loved him.

God. How he'd wanted to tell her anything and everything she wanted to hear.

What did she want to hear from him now? What could he say now that she'd believe? That he loved her? That he had always loved her?

She wouldn't believe him. Not now, with her life torn apart, her confidence in the cellar. She wouldn't even look at him, let him see her face. She was wounded, mind and body. She was weak, defeated. If he told her he loved her, she'd hate him, and he wouldn't blame her.

"I...I'm sorry," Sophie said, pushing herself away from him, bending down to pick up her cane. She took the square-folded blue-and-white handkerchief he offered her and wiped her eyes, blew her nose. "I don't do this, Riv. I never do this. And yet, it's all I've been doing this whole damn day."

"It had to happen sometime, Sophie," he said, believing himself to be very reasonable.

Her head shot up. "Why? Why did it have to happen?"

River felt about as helpless as a man trying to whistle a wild stallion to heel. "Why? Because you were mugged, Soph. You were injured, you've broken your engagement, you—''

Sophie raised her hands and turned her head, as if shielding herself from his words. "No. I know all that. I know *what* happened. I want to know *why* it happened. Why to *me?*''

River was nonplussed. Of all the questions she might have asked, it had never occurred to him that she'd ask this one. "Why not you?" he responded, a man who had been a child of so much unhappiness that it had ceased to amaze him when the world didn't run the way it did on the television sitcoms. "Do you think you have some sort of immunity to the bad stuff? How do you do that, Soph? Take a shot for it, like with measles? Man, wouldn't there be a long line for that immunization shot. It would probably stretch halfway around the world.''

She looked at him for long moments, then blinked, lowered her eyelids, shook her head. "How do you do it, Riv? How do you make it all sound so simple? Except now I'm a whining idiot, aren't I? Poor little Sophie.''

"You're not an idiot, Sophie," River told her, squeezing her shoulders. "You've been knocked down. Now you've got to take it easy for a while, get your strength back and give yourself some time to heal. You'll be back in fighting form before you know it.''

"I don't know," Sophie said, sighing. "I think all the fight's gone out of me. I feel so useless, so used…so ugly and undesirable. I mean, even my own mother says—''

"Aw, hell, Sophie," River said, pulling her closer, wanting to shake her, wake her up, shock her out of her despair. "Does this look like you're undesirable?"

He slanted his mouth against hers, gripped her shoulders so that she couldn't move away from him. He kissed her in anger, with a desire he'd fought as long as he could remember, with a hunger that clawed through his body.

She stiffened, resisted, but only for the length of a heartbeat. Then the cane hit the ground and her arms were around him, her fingernails gripping his back through his denim shirt. Her mouth opened under his and he plundered her with his tongue, slipped one jean-clad leg between her thighs, fused her to him from mouth to hip.

Let her father comfort her. Let her doctors reassure her. But the only way to make her forget what she saw in her mirror, and the words Meredith had lashed her with so painfully, was to *show* her how desirable she was to him. How very much he wanted her.

He wasn't gentle. She didn't need to be treated as if she was fragile, an invalid. She needed to know that she was a woman, a woman this man needed.

He kissed her, kiss after drugging kiss, each one longer, deeper than the one that came before it, so that his heart pounded, his ears buzzed and he lost all thought of time or place...or the years and circumstances that divided them.

Slipping an arm under her knees, he lifted her high against his chest, still kissing her, branding her throat and the V of skin above her blouse with his lips. He carried her inside the stable, moving through the darkness, past the softly blowing horses, to the birthing stall lined with sweet fresh hay in anticipation of one of the ranch's prize mares foaling in the next day or so.

River went to his knees, then laid Sophie on a bed of straw and followed her down as she reached her arms up to him, her eyes squeezed shut, her breath coming quickly, her mouth slightly open as she tried to regulate her breathing.

He didn't want her to regulate her breathing, catch her breath in any way at all. Because then she might think, give him time to think.

This was not the time for thinking. This was the time for actions to take the place of words, for want and need that had been repressed for so long to explode and take control.

He kissed her again, even as his fingers fumbled with the buttons of her blouse, worked to pull her shirttail out of her jeans. His mouth left hers, traveled down her slim form. His tongue trailed down over her breasts, and he pressed kisses against her flat midriff even as he worked to open the front closure of her bra.

Then her breasts were free, and he claimed them with hands and mouth, fingers and tongue. He felt her raise up from the straw so that he could touch her, learn her, feel her swell against his palm, stiffen against his tongue.

Sophie held him tightly, dragging her hands over his back, tugging at the denim as if longing for the feel of his skin but unable to do anything about removing his shirt.

River went back on his heels, grabbed the lapels of his shirt and ripped it off, fighting his way out of the long sleeves then throwing the ruined shirt across the stall. Sophie moaned, and reached for him again as he yanked off his boots. She unzipped her jeans as he opened his belt buckle and rid himself of his jeans and his briefs.

They were in the dark. Hot and tense and yearning in the dark. Coming together with an urgency that stripped them of inhibitions, revealed the core of their desire, an almost animal heat that could not be denied.

Until River got slapped in the head by a belated dose of common sense. He stilled, his hand cupping Sophie's hip, his long legs tangled with hers, his mouth against her ear. ''Damn,'' he whispered. ''Damn, damn, *damn.*''

Sophie was still kissing him, tasting him, exploring his upper body with her hands. It took her a few moments to realize that he'd gone still in her arms, had begun slowly withdrawing his body from her reach.

''What?'' she asked, half sitting up, reaching for him in the darkness. ''What's wrong?''

River scrubbed at his face with both hands. ''I…I'm not…prepared.'' When she remained quiet, he tried to peer down at her, but it was too dark to see her face.

Darkness, however, didn't keep him from hearing her. ''You're not— Oh, Riv, that's so wonderful.''

He turned his back on her. ''*Wonderful?* How in hell could you think—''

Sophie sat up completely, pressed her cheek against his back. "Face it, Riv, it would be a lot less wonderful if you carried a gross of the things around with you in your wallet, like you were hoping to get lucky every night of the week."

River let his head drop toward his chest, his long hair falling forward around his face. "Only you, Sophie. Only you could see this as a *good* thing. But it is, you know. We shouldn't even be here."

She pulled away from him and gave him a two-handed push in the back. "Oh, really? Is that right, Riv? Joe's little girl and the charity foster child? Is that it? Because if it is, you've been playing that record too damn long, and I'm sick of it."

"I never said—"

"No, you never said," Sophie agreed, pulling at his shoulders, forcing him to turn and face her. "But I knew, Riv. I always knew. You could have had me all those years ago. You could have been my first, my last. And now here we are, lying in the straw like teenagers, and you've dreamed up another excuse. Did it ever occur to you that you really *don't* want me? That I was just the forbidden fruit you could dream about and never have to do anything about? I ran, Riv, I know I ran. But you *hid*. You hid, and now you're here because you pity me. Well, let me tell you something, River James, I don't want your pity. And I don't want you."

She reached for her blouse, feeling for it in the straw, a sob escaping her lips as she struggled to locate her bra.

River lifted his hands, trying to grasp something he

couldn't quite see, couldn't quite hold. An answer. A reason. Something. "I don't pity you, Soph," he said at last. "I want you so bad it hurts."

"Oh, really? Well, you have a damn funny way of showing it, Riv, because I've never felt *less* wanted in my life."

Those were either the right words or the wrong words—he'd figure that out later—because they spurred River into grabbing hold of Sophie's forearms as she tried to push them into her bra straps. "I want you, Sophie. I do want you."

"Then prove it, Riv. Prove it. Lose your mind, lose control, and for once in your life *do* something without worrying about consequences." She moved forward, pressed her mouth against his. "Don't let me leave here, Riv. Please don't let me leave here like this."

He let go of her forearms, gathered her into his arms and deepened their kiss as they fell, together, back onto the sweet straw.

Dr. Martha Wilkes leaned back in her chair and looked out over her Jackson, Mississippi, neighborhood of pretty little houses on a pretty little street.

She shouldn't be here, at least not in her role as a psychologist specializing in repressed memory. She should be in her impersonal downtown office, where she could keep up her own defenses as she carefully, skillfully broke down those of her patients, getting them to open up, talk to her—really talk to her—and fight through the accumulated baggage of a lifetime, to the truth.

But she was here, at only seven in the morning, still sipping on her first cup of coffee, dressed casually, without hose or heels, watching Louise Smith pace the oriental carpet.

Dr. Wilkes liked Louise. Really liked her. She'd come into the office for the first time almost five years ago, frightened, withdrawn, obviously carrying more than just baggage. She'd come in stumbling under the weight of a steamer trunk of trouble.

Louise was a pretty woman, a woman whose problems somehow didn't show in her face, unless you looked deeply into her soft brown eyes. Then a person could see a depth of despair that would stagger someone stronger than Louise, sometimes still did stagger the woman.

Like this morning, when Louise had phoned and begged for an immediate appointment.

"Someone needs me, Dr. Wilkes," Louise said now, turning toward the psychologist. "I can feel it. I'm needed somewhere."

Dr. Wilkes sighed. Not a good thing to do, sigh. Not in front of a patient. Even if Louise was much more than a patient. She was a friend. Their sessions may have begun all those years ago as strictly professional, but their relationship had evolved into something deeper, more personal.

And that was wrong. Dr. Wilkes knew it. She had stepped over the line, become too involved with Louise's problems. Maybe today was the day to pull back, restate the obvious and get them back onto that less level doctor–patient playing field.

"Sit down, Louise," Dr. Wilkes said, motioning to

a small, comfortable upholstered chair near the op- posite side of the cozily furnished room. She watched as Louise ran a hand over her simply cut light brown hair, smoothed her hands down the sides of her neat cotton dress that skimmed a trim body that also belied Louise's fifty-two years.

"Let's recap, okay?" the doctor said, reaching for Louise's file, a file she knew almost by heart.

Louise sat very still, her spine erect, her hands neatly folded in her lap, her legs crossed at the ankles. Every inch the lady. "If you think it will help, Doctor, certainly. And again, I apologize for disturbing you at home. It's just that these past few days the dreams have become so vivid."

"Yes, as you said." Dr. Wilkes opened the file on the desk in front of her. "All right. You were born Patricia Portman, fifty-two years ago, in California."

"At least we think so," Louise inserted, sighing. "Isn't it odd? That we've never checked for a birth certificate, not in all these years?"

"Not odd, Louise. Frustrating. You wouldn't per- mit me to check any deeper, to consult anything more than the medical records that accompanied you upon your discharge from St. James Clinic."

"*Both* of my discharges from St. James Clinic," Louise corrected.

Dr. Wilkes shook her head, not in dissent, but be- cause this had been the largest stumbling block she faced with Louise. The woman had first shown up in Jackson, then disappeared, and then reappeared a few years later, both times upon her discharge from St. James Clinic in California. The doctor knew Louise's

life for the past thirty years, but nothing of her life
before she'd entered the California prison system.

And Louise refused to allow a search that probed
any more deeply into her complicated past, a past
Louise still swore not to remember.

"Why, Louise? Why won't you let me learn more
about your background? We could locate your parents, possibly some siblings, relatives, who could help
us understand—"

Louise's chin lifted. "Help us? You saw the records, Dr. Wilkes. I was in that asylum for years.
Years. And never once a visitor, never a single contact
or inquiry from anyone. If I have relatives, they're
either dead or I'm dead to them. They believe I killed
Ellis Mayfair."

Dr. Wilkes pinched the bridge of her nose between
thumb and forefinger. "Louise, you *did* kill Ellis
Mayfair. You went to prison for killing him, and then
to St. James Clinic because your deteriorating mental
health made it impossible for you to continue living
with the general prison population. You were re-
leased, supposedly cured, only to show up on the
grounds again a few years later, injured, disoriented,
completely out of your head. Six months later, you
were back here, although how you traveled from
Jackson to California, and *why,* remains a mystery."

Louise shook her head, squeezed her eyes shut.
"No. No, that's wrong. That's always been wrong. I
didn't kill that man. I didn't know that man."

Was this the right time to push Louise? How hard
could she push her without sending the woman back
to that dark place she had been hiding from for the

nine years since her second release from St. James, for all of the five years she'd been under her treatment?

"Louise, you had an illegitimate child with Ellis Mayfair, a child he took from you as you slept after giving birth in a motel room. A child he destroyed, or sold. We'll never know exactly what happened, because with Ellis there, and the child gone, you flew into a rage and you killed Ellis Mayfair."

Louise bent forward, covering her head with her hands. "Oh, God. God, help me, please help me. My poor baby. I don't remember. I don't remember..."

Dr. Wilkes pressed her lips together and looked around her small study. Her gaze drifted to the wooden sculpture of an African mother and child. She'd never had a child, had chosen never to have a child, but she could see the love in the expression on that mother's face, and could hear in Louise's sobs the sorrow of a mother denied.

"When you phoned, you said something about a child, Louise. About a child who needed you."

Louise lifted her head, withdrew a pristine white linen square from her pocket and wiped her eyes.

Dr. Wilkes hid a small smile. Louise was such a lady, from her head to her toes. Her movements were graceful, refined, her posture always perfect, her personal hygiene the best. A real lady.

Dr. Wilkes felt that same refinement, and knew some of it had grown from her environment, and that some of it was developed as her own special protection. It wasn't easy being a woman in her specialized professional field, and it was never easy being a black woman in any field.

So Dr. Wilkes saw a lot of herself in Louise Smith, even though they were two very different people from very different worlds. Louise was trying, desperately trying, to find herself, understand herself, help herself. Dr. Wilkes had slowly, painfully, carved out a professional niche, and then worked—perhaps too hard—to protect it.

Give it any name, dissect it any way, and the bottom line remained the same for both women. They had a lot to protect, a lot to fear. And fear was a common denominator.

"Louise," Dr. Wilkes said after a few moments, "have I ever told you how much I admire you?"

Louise refolded her small handkerchief and slipped it back into her pocket. "Admire me? Why would you do that? I'm a murderer, remember?"

"You're a *survivor,* Louise," Dr. Wilkes corrected. "You came back here a second time from St. James Clinic, confused and alone, and you made something of yourself. You worked, you worked hard, and you've risen into a responsible position at the university, own your own small home. Many people—most people—would consider yours a most remarkable success story."

"Most people don't have my nightmares," Louise said, sighing. She squeezed her hands into fists. "I just feel this *need* inside me. Someone needs me, and I need him."

"Him? I thought you came here to talk about the

child? The records show that you'd said it was a girl child.''

"Yes, yes, a girl. There's a girl. Perhaps more than one. Children. So many children. Perhaps I worked as a teacher or in a nursery school? Why do I feel there are so many children who need me?"

"Overcompensation," Dr. Wilkes said quietly. "Longing for the infant Mayfair stole from you, all the unborn children he took from your future. You would have made a wonderful mother, Louise, and you fill your empty arms with dreams of those children you never held, will never hold."

"And the man? I dream of a man, Dr. Wilkes. A man who comes to me in this beautiful garden. I'm on my hands and knees, digging in the rich earth, listening to the sound of a fountain in the near distance. Warm sun on my head, the calming tinkle of falling water, the smell of saltwater in the breeze. I hear him approach, turn to see him, shielding my eyes against the glare of the sun. He's there. Tall, strong. But the sun obscures his face. I don't recognize him, and he turns away. I call after him. 'Wait,' I call to him. 'Please wait!'''

She pressed a hand to her mouth for a few moments, as if holding back a scream. "And then I wake up. The garden is gone, the man is gone, and all I hear is the pounding of my own heart. My broken, empty heart."

Dr. Wilkes got up, poured a glass of water for each of them and handed one to Louise. "Hypnosis, Louise. I know you don't want it, have fought it for years, but we're running out of options here, my dear. I want to see who else lives inside you. Because you're not in there alone, Louise. You know it, and I know it. You've changed your name, but you're still Patricia Portman. You have to find out who Patricia Portman was before you can truly close that door and let Louise get on with her life. You've changed your name, you've locked away another personality, perhaps more than one.''

Louise refused the glass, got up, and began pacing once more. ''I can't believe that. I can't believe I'm some Sybil, hiding multiple personalities inside my head, letting one out at a time, becoming someone else. Someone evil.''

''You say you didn't kill Ellis Mayfair, Louise. That you couldn't have done such a thing. And yet the prison record that traveled here with you from St. James Clinic clearly shows that it was your fingerprints that were on the pieces of broken lamp you used to knock him unconscious. Your fingerprints were on the scissors stuck in his chest. His blood was on your hands when the police found you.''

''No. It wasn't me. It wasn't me.''

''Then who was it, Louise? Who else is inside your head? Who did this to you—got you locked up, had you committed to a mental institution, not once, but twice. Where did you disappear to after your first move to Jackson? How did you end up back in California, back at St. James? Fill in the blanks for me, Louise. Tell me what you know.''

Louise subsided into the chair once more. ''I don't know anything. I'm what you tell me, what the prison and St. James records tell me. And if there's another

me inside my head—a horrible person, a murderer—
I can't let her out again. I've accepted my past as
much as I can, even as I don't remember it. But I
can't let that other person, that evil me, be a part of
my future. So, no, Dr. Wilkes. I'm sorry, but no. No
hypnosis. No regression.''

"And no answers,'' Dr. Wilkes said, sighing.
"These nightmares, Louise, these headaches that
bring you to your knees. They're not going away.
They're becoming more frequent, more intense.
Surely you see that something has to be done? Drastic
measures yes, but in a controlled environment. I
wouldn't do anything to hurt you, Louise. Haven't we
come far enough for you to trust me?''

Louise looked up at the psychologist, her doctor,
her friend. "Why couldn't the other me be a better
me? I wouldn't mind meeting a better me.''

"You *are* that better you, Louise,'' Dr. Wilkes said
kindly, putting a hand on Louise's shoulder. "You've
beaten down the disturbed, unhappy personality that
destroyed your past. You don't even need any medication anymore. But, my dear, unless you can face
that past, face *all* of it, come to grips with it, I'm
afraid these nightmares of yours will never end.
Please. At least consider hypnosis.''

Louise wet her dry lips, nodded. "I...I'll consider
it.''

Six

Sophie woke slowly, a small smile playing about her mouth as she snuggled more deeply under the covers and did her best to hold on to a fantastic dream where she felt loved and desired. River was with her, her own Riv, the person she had loved as both a boy and a man.

He held her, he kissed her, he claimed her. He took her higher, higher, their mutual desire feeding on the flames of need, of want...until that blessed release, that mutual explosion that had been like nothing she'd ever experienced, ever dreamed she could experience. An awakening. A rocket trip to the moon, the stars. And all with Riv's arms around her, his body melded against hers, into hers; deeply inside her, filling her, exploding within her. It had been a stolen moment, a dream in which her lone wolf had come to her, loved her...

Her eyes snapped open wide and she sat up in the bed, raked her fingers through her hair.

No. It hadn't been a dream. It had happened.

"Oh, God, what have I done?" Sophie groaned, falling back against the pillows. "Riv, what the hell have we done?"

She pressed her hands to her chest, willing her heartbeat to slow, marshaling her thoughts, attempting to think rationally about a truly irrational situation. An impulsive act, one she had goaded him into, dared him into.

"Because I'm out of my tiny mind," she told herself in a hoarse whisper. "What in *hell* was I thinking?"

But that was the whole point. She hadn't thought, hadn't wanted to think. She'd been bruised and battered. She'd been marked, scarred. She needed to feel desirable, needed to have someone hold her, tell her she was beautiful, prove that she could still have a life, still have dreams.

She'd told herself she had gone down to the stables to see the horses, to get away from the family, to be alone.

She'd lied to herself.

She'd gone down to the stables to see River. To use him as a sort of whipping post, to pour out her fears and frustrations, her anger and her despair. Hadn't that been what she'd always done? Run to Riv. Dumped on Riv. Let Riv make it all better.

She'd *used* him. She used him so badly, goaded

him past all endurance. Wept on his shoulder, clung to him, used her body to tempt him, used their memories to draw him in, make him willing to do anything—anything—that would stop her tears, heal her hurt.

How he must hate her this morning. How justified he would be to hate her.

She hated herself.

"Now there's something not entirely new," she told herself, shaking her head. "You've been your own worst enemy for some time now, haven't you? Poor Sophie. Poor, poor, stupid Sophie."

A knock on the door broke into her self-pity, startling her. Blinking in surprise, Sophie turned and looked at the door to the hallway. She panicked. Could it be River? Her mother? She didn't want to face either of them. "Yes? Who is it?"

The doorknob turned and the door slowly opened, Emily Blair Colton's chestnut-red head peeked into the room. "It's okay to come in? I didn't want to wake you, but it is almost noon, you know."

"I—I had a late night," Sophie said, watching as her sister came fully into the room. Emily was eight years her junior, and had been adopted by Joe and Meredith as a toddler. A cute baby, with bright red curls and a happy, smiling face. A giggle that had delighted everyone. It had been an eleven-year-old Emily who had been in the automobile accident with Meredith, and it was Emily who seemed the most affected by that accident. Not physically. No, she'd come out of the accident with only minor injuries.

But something had happened that day. To Meredith. To Emily.

The same something that had happened to all of the Colton family in the weeks and months and years after that accident, as Meredith changed, became distant, strange…and life on the ranch built for "joy" had gone dark and cold.

Now Emily was all grown up, her fire-engine-red curls now a more subdued chestnut, thick and wavy as it fell down past her shoulders. She still had those same huge blue eyes, that same sweet and pretty face, those same dimples in her cheeks. But she was all grown up, and she had changed.

"Yes," Emily said now, sitting down on the bottom of the bed, "I guess you did have a late night. I stopped by your room twice, and knocked, but you didn't answer. I missed you at dinner. We all did."

"You *all* did, Em? Now why do I doubt that? Why do I very seriously doubt that?"

"Mom," Emily said, bowing her head. "You mean Mom, don't you?"

"Congratulations, Em, you made it past the preliminary round and into the finals. Now, would you like to see what's behind door number two?" Sophie asked, then deliberately lifted her chin, pulled back her hair, and turned her left cheek toward Emily.

Emily was all grown up in many ways, but she was still young, only nineteen, and she still had this way of often saying exactly what came into her head. "Oh, wow. He really got you, didn't he?"

Sophie let her hair fall back into place, wishing it longer, so that it could become a shoulder-length curtain covering the entire side of her face. "Yeah, Em. He really got me."

"Damn, Sophie, I'm *so* sorry," Emily apologized quickly. "I didn't mean that. It's not bad, not bad at all. And Dad says you'll be having plastic surgery soon. It's just that I hadn't expected it to be so long. I mean, that's a big slice. You could have been killed. And you had to have been terrified."

"To tell you the truth, Emily, I think I was too mad to be terrified. That took a little while, until after I was safe. Then, well, then I sort of fell apart. Into tiny, itty-bitty pieces, as a matter of fact."

Emily nodded. "You broke up with Chet. Yes, I heard. And took a leave of absence from your company. Well, you know, I think those were good things, Sophie."

Sophie smiled ruefully. "You're glad I broke up with Chet? Really?"

Emily was and always had been one of the most honest people Sophie had ever known, and she was sure she wouldn't disappoint her now by hedging or saying something silly and meaningless. "Yes, Sophie, really. You'll be much better off with River. Everyone knows that."

Okay, so Emily hadn't disappointed her. She had, however, shocked her. "River? *Everyone* knows that?"

Nodding, Emily continued, "Oh, sure. You should have seen him after you and Chet left after announcing your engagement during the Christmas holiday. Stomping around, kicking things, taking off into the hills for a week without telling anyone if or when he'd be back. Inez told me he'd been the same way when you first left for college. Mean and snarly and telling anyone who asked him what was wrong to just mind their own damn business.''

Sophie shifted slightly on the mattress, moving so that she sat cross-legged, her hands on her ankles. ''River doesn't like to lose, that's all. I think he much preferred to have me following him around, mooning over him like some lovesick calf. That's all, and it's a far cry from the kind of love you're talking about, let me tell you.''

Emily shrugged. ''If you say so, Soph,'' she said, then changed the subject. ''Have you heard about the party? Mom's throwing this big sixtieth-birthday bash for Dad. Dad's not happy about it, but Mom's over the moon, planning menus and motifs, hiring bands, stuff like that. All Dad keeps saying is that he thought he'd only have to wear a monkey suit again to marry off one of us kids.''

''Poor Dad.'' Sophie shook her head. ''How did he let her talk him into it? Wait, never mind. I already know. Dad just found it easier to give in, right?''

''The story of our lives, at least for almost the past decade,'' Emily agreed.

''The good mommy and the bad mommy, huh, Sparrow,'' Sophie said quietly, then sighed.

''Or, to be precise, the good mommy and the *evil* mommy. Yes, and I wish I'd never said that to anyone. But, hey, I was what—eleven? All I knew was that I woke up, saw two of her, and then pretty much spazzed out, went a little nuts. I wouldn't let Mom in my room, wouldn't let her touch me. Had those screaming nightmares. You're right, Mom used to call me her little sparrow. But her little sparrow turned into a screeching hyena. I must have been a real treat. I still have nightmares, more now than I did when I was a kid. And she knows about them.''

"Still, Emily? Oh, I'm so sorry." Sophie got out from under the covers and moved down the bed, to put a hand on Emily's arm. "But that didn't and doesn't mean that Mom should turn away from you, practically cut you off from her life the way she did. It wasn't you who pushed her away, not really. She pushed herself away, from all of us. When I came home after my first semester at college, it was as if I'd walked into a totally different house. Dad acting as distant as he had after Michael died, Mom always going off somewhere, shopping, then giving parties every night of the holidays. Everyone else just sort of walking around, going through the motions…and with the heart gone out of everyone. I'd never realized how important Mom was to all of us, to our happiness, until she went away.''

"Gone without being gone," Emily agreed, then shook herself, took a deep breath. "Well, that's not why I'm in here, you know. I'm here to tell you that Inez is setting up a cold buffet lunch on the patio and expects everyone to be there with appetite in hand in—'' she looked down at her watch ''—about fifteen minutes. So chop, chop, Soph. This is one meal you aren't going to miss, because if you do, you'd better be ready for all of us to come knocking down this door. Brothers and sisters exploding into the room. It wouldn't be a pretty picture.''

"Okay, you've convinced me," Sophie said, laughing as she left the bed, favoring her right leg slightly, and went over to her dresser for clean underwear in preparation of heading for the shower. "Who all is here?"

Emily held up one hand and began ticking off her fingers with her other hand. "We've got Drake, who finds any excuse to hang around Inez's Maya whenever he's home on leave, although nobody is supposed to notice that. Trust me, Inez has noticed, and she's not happy about it, not with Drake going off playing navy SEAL every time we think he'll be home for a while. We've also got Rand, who showed up with a briefcase bulging with legal papers for Dad to sign. We *had* Amber, who decided she'd rather spend the day helping out over at Hopechest Ranch, holding up Mom's end now that Mom is busy finding new ways to spend Dad's money. We've got— Nope, River rode out early this morning, to check out a mare on the next ranch. So that's it. Except for Liza. She's here for a short visit before she goes out on tour, which she doesn't want to do, by the way. Still, with that voice of hers, it would be a crime to hide so much talent under a bushel, right? Anyway we're heading into Prosperino after lunch, to the hairdresser. Want to come along? I'm sure they could fit you in."

"No thanks, Em. I'm letting my hair grow," Sophie said, reaching into her closet for a lime green skirt and blouse. "So, not quite a full house, huh? Is it just Liza, or are Uncle Graham and Aunt Cynthia here, too?"

"Man, you really don't come home often, do you?

Uncle Graham and Aunt Cynthia in the same room, at the same time? Hardly, Soph. Besides, although it used to be that they ignored Liza and Jackson, now it's the other way around, at least for Liza. She avoids her parents like the plague, both of them. Aunt Cynthia because she keeps trying to manage Liza's career, but most especially Uncle Graham. It's like he's...I don't know...*disappointed* her in some way. Not that she talks about it.''

"Dad's brother has never been very approachable, or fatherly. Still, that's too bad, all the way around. Isn't it enough that our branch of the Colton family is falling apart? I'm glad Liza has you, Em, and that you have her.''

"Yeah,'' Emily said, hopping down from the bed and giving Sophie a kiss on the cheek. "She's like the older sister I never had.''

"Why, you—'' Sophie countered, giving Emily a friendly swipe with her skirt and blouse. "You were my kid sister. I was honor bound to ignore you once you'd started to grow up and ceased to be cute and cuddly. Or am I to forget the times you got into my makeup, or the time you told River that I'd written 'Mrs. River James' inside my diary fifty times?''

Emily laughed, then cupped a hand to her ear, pretended to be listening for something. "Did you hear that? I heard that. It's Inez, muttering under her breath that she doesn't cook for her health, she cooks because she expects people to eat. Gotta go. See you in a few?''

"See you in a few,'' Sophie answered, heading for the bathroom attached to her room. Once in the shower, she tipped back her head to keep the sting of the shower off her healing cut, let the water pour down over her body. The body River had touched. Kissed. Awakened.

She felt so alive, and yet so dead inside, where it really mattered. She reached for the liquid soap and the nylon net scrubbie, performing her ablutions quickly, impersonally, trying to forget that River's touch had branded her forever, changed her forever.

River's expert touch on the reins guided his mount down a narrow path running through a series of small cliffs and outcroppings, all the way to the beach below. He dismounted, found a rock large enough to hold down the reins so the horse wouldn't wander. Then he set off across the rocks, toward the waves crashing against them, sending up a white, wild spray that had been beating against this same beach since the beginning of time.

He sat down on the large boulder he'd claimed as his thinking place years ago, when he'd first come to the ranch. His back to the cliffs, he propped his outstretched arm on his bent knee, tipped back his cowboy hat and tried to stare down the waves.

This ocean could be angry, turning gray and menacing, whitecaps forming well out to sea, hurling itself against the rocks in a fury. This ocean could be calm, gentle. Welcoming. No matter the weather, the season, this ocean was a promise. A promise that it would always be here, steadily doing its job, making its moves, holding firm against time and man and bending only to the phases of the moon.

He looked up at the sky, a wide, nearly cloudless sky, bluer than blue, with a bright yellow sun that had already begun its daily slide toward the horizon, as it had somehow gone past four o'clock, the day slipping away from him.

He'd never brought anyone here to this place. Not even Sophie. Especially not Sophie, at least not when they'd both been younger. It had been the one place he could go without her following, his one safe haven from her chatter, her persistence, his own awareness of her as she'd grown up. It had been the place where he hid his amused affection, his flattered ego at the way she pursued him, his love for his "little sister" that had turned into something much deeper, much more dangerous.

Gulls circled overhead, laughing at him, their piercing cries mocking him because he felt he was safe here. He wasn't safe here, he wasn't safe anywhere. Not anymore, and probably not for a long, long time.

He loved Sophie Colton. Loved her, adored her, desired her, wanted and needed her more than he did air to breathe, food to eat. He'd loved her for so long, denied that love for so long, but he had to face facts now.

He loved her. He'd made love to her. Wildly, recklessly, irresponsibly.

And there was no going back.

"No going back," he said into the wind that swirled up from the water, "and not much in front of you except Sophie's face as she left you last night. Sophie's pinched mouth. Sophie's eyes, that hid from you as she dressed, limped away without looking back. And what did you do? Nothing. What did you say? Nothing. Oh, yeah, James. You've blown it. You've blown it big this time.''

Sophie stood at the very top of the cliff, the long grass waving against her bare legs, leaning heavily on her cane after the long walk from the road. She shouldn't have driven the car; her knee wasn't up to working the pedals, and she'd nearly come to grief once she'd given up and begun to work the gas and brake with her left foot.

But she had to come, she had to see...and she'd been right. River sat on the rocks, down at the beach. He sat so still, like some sort of living statue, his back to her, to the world, as he searched the endless horizon for answers to questions only he knew.

She'd known about this place forever, had followed River there several times, but she had never climbed down the rocky path, never interrupted his solitude. She didn't know why, because she'd seemed to make it her personal mission to invade every area of his life ever since he first came to live with them on the ranch. But even a younger, more impulsive Sophie had somehow known that this was a special place, a private place.

River's special, private place.

What was he thinking now? What questions was he asking of the sun, the sea? Was he thinking about leaving the ranch, leaving her? Was he kicking himself for what had happened between them last night? Did he blame himself?

Or did he blame her?

At lunch, her dad had informed her that he'd set up a three-days-a-week physical therapy session for her in Prosperino, and that River would be driving her into town for the sessions, the first of which was already scheduled for the following day. She'd protested, said she could drive herself to town on her own, but to no avail.

Is that why she'd driven the car? No, it wasn't. Because, if all she'd wanted to do was prove that she could drive, she could have driven anywhere. But she hadn't driven anywhere, she'd driven straight here, where she instinctively knew River would be, sitting beside the ocean, thinking his thoughts.

"Don't go, Riv," she whispered under her breath. "I was going to go, run away yet again. But I can't. I have to stay this time. I have to face what's going on with Mom, with Dad. I have to stay for Emily, for all of us. And I have to stay for you, even if you don't want me, even if you regret what we did. I have to stay, Riv, and so do you. We have to know what happens next, don't we, Riv? What happens to us, if there even is an us. We have to know."

Seven

Rand Colton picked up the small pile of papers, tapped them against the table to arrange them, then placed them back inside his briefcase. "So, that's it. I don't know how I forgot to bring these papers with me yesterday. Oh, well. Another day, another tree sacrificed in the almighty name of multiple copies. Did you ever notice? We're in the computer age, or so we say, and yet sometimes it seems like all computers have done is make it easier to print out more paper. Right, Dad? Dad? Are you okay?"

Joe Colton lifted his head and looked at his oldest son. "What? Oh yeah, yeah. I'm fine. Rand? Did you know that Drake has been seeing Maya? Inez is pretty upset about it."

"Drake and Maya? Really?"

"Really, although nobody is supposed to know. Of

course, everyone does, we're just not talking about it.''

"The elephant in the living room. We've had a lot of elephants around here," Rand said, nodding his head as he snapped his briefcase closed and set it on the patio beside his chair. "But what's the problem, anyway? I thought Inez liked my little brother."

Joe took a sip of lemonade, then held the chilled glass between his hands. "She does. So does Marco. But they worry about their daughter and don't want to see her hurt. Being a navy SEAL is not exactly a nine-to-five job, you know. Or as safe as, say, being a lawyer.''

"Oh, I don't know about that," Rand said, grinning. "Being a lawyer can be mighty dangerous. Just think of all the paper cuts."

Joe smiled, shook his head. "You're not helping, Rand. And seriously, do you think I should speak to Drake?"

"What does Mom— Well, never mind about that," Rand said quickly. "But no, I don't think you should say anything. Drake and Maya are both adults. They'll do what they want to do, no matter what anyone says."

Joe put down the glass, leaned back in his chair. "That's what I think, too. Okay, on to the next subject. Have you seen Sophie?"

"I did. At lunch yesterday, remember? Seen her, talked to her, and come away worried about her," Rand told his father. "I guess I'm just not used to seeing her without a smile on her face. Is she going to be all right?"

"They say time heals all wounds," Joe remarked, sighing.

"And wounds all heels," Rand agreed, nodding. "Speaking of which, I just got the police report on the mugger this morning, but thought I'd speak to you about it first, before saying anything to Sophie. He fits Sophie's description, except for one thing. He's very dead. Drug overdose. He was found in an alley only six or so blocks from where Sophie got mugged, but it took a while for the police to make the connection."

"Damn," Joe said, shaking his head. "I don't know if that's a good thing or a bad thing. Sophie may have wanted to face him in court."

"I doubt it, Dad. This way is best. Another door closed, another reason to feel safer about moving on, getting on with her life. And, speaking of Sophie's life, how's River? Do you think the two of them might get it right this time?"

"I hope so. I asked him to drive her to her physical therapy sessions in Prosperino three days a week, and he didn't say no. That's where they are now. And if that doesn't work, I might try locking the two of them in the same room for a few days, until they finally figure out what the rest of us know. Chet Wallace? What was the child thinking? Although, to be fair, I have the feeling good old Chet was already halfway out the door before Sophie's...incident."

"At least halfway out the door, probably farther than that," Rand agreed, but didn't elaborate. "Well," he said, bracing his hands against the arms of the chair and rising to his feet. "Since she wasn't at lunch yesterday, and since I have to leave soon, I guess I should go find Mom, say hello.''

''That would be nice,'' Joe said, also rising. ''She's no doubt on the phone planning the party.''

''It's going to be a real bash, isn't it? Are you okay with that?''

''If it makes your mother happy,'' Joe said, following after his son.

Twenty feet away, on the other side of some tall bushes, a casement window slowly wound closed and Meredith Colton turned away from the bedroom window, a smile on her face.

It was going to happen. The party was going to happen. Joe was too old, too tired, to fight her on this, on anything.

Still, he was a problem, and he wasn't as easy to manage anymore.

Meredith was certain Sophie's mugging had a lot to do with this new hint of spine she saw in Joe, this reawakening realization of how dissatisfied he was with his life. He might even try to send her away again, as he'd done when she'd first told him about Teddy.

That crack the other night—about her being the mother of children, but not all of them his had been nasty. But when he'd asked her if she was insane, mad? That had been the topper. How dare he question her sanity? If she hadn't been sure before, she was now. And she would do what she had to do, to protect herself, to protect her boys.

She made a mental note to consider Donna Karan for her widow's weeds.

"I still don't see why it has to be you," Sophie said, sitting as close to the passenger door as possible as River drove the SUV toward Prosperino.

"Yes, it was good for me, too," River replied tightly.

Sophie turned her head, glared at him. Of all the things he could have said, for his first words to her since she'd left him in the stables, he had picked ones sure to incense her. That man was uncanny, knew just what buttons to push. "That's not what I meant, damn it."

"I know, Soph, but we had to talk about it some time. Or am I supposed to develop some sort of convenient amnesia?"

"It would be nice. Why don't you work on that?" Sophie muttered, sinking lower on her spine as the scenery flashed by on either side of the highway. "Because it's not going to happen again."

"Oh, absolutely. I've taken a vow of chastity, as a matter of fact. However, if you could stop moving around on that seat and looking so damned sexy, I'd really appreciate it."

Sophie sat up once more, smoothed her hands over her nylon sweatpants. "Sexy? Like this? All dressed up and ready for physical therapy? You know, Riv, I'm beginning to think you may have some hormonal imbalance that clouds your judgment. Maybe you ought to consider cold showers."

"Maybe I ought to consider taking you over my

knee, the way I did when you were fifteen, and I caught you snooping around in my room.''

Sophie rolled her eyes. ''And I told you—I was just trying to find out your shirt size, so I could get you a new shirt for your birthday. And it didn't hurt, by the way.''

River turned to her, grinned. ''Did so. It had to. You had such a skinny butt. Not that you do now.''

''Are you insinuating that I'm fat? Well, let me tell you, River James, there is absolutely nothing the matter with my— Oh, forget it! Just drive the damn car, all right?''

River chuckled under his breath. They were both silent for the remainder of the drive, until River parked the SUV, then turned to her before she could get out. ''How long, Soph?'' he asked, holding on to her forearm.

''How long? How long for what? The therapy? About an hour, I suppose.''

''Okay. But, no, that's not what I meant. How long, Soph, before you can tell?''

Sophie lowered her eyelids, bit her bottom lip. ''I don't know. Two weeks or so, I guess. We did a commercial for one of the new tests, and they're supposedly ninety-five percent accurate very early on.'' She lifted her head and stared at him. ''But that's not going to happen, so you don't have to worry about it, okay?''

He nodded, his eyes shaded by the ever-present cowboy hat, and she escaped from the car, heading toward the rehabilitation center.

It wasn't going to happen? Had she sounded convincing? Was he informed enough to realize that she'd said she'd know in about two weeks—and that her admission meant she had been smack in the middle of her cycle, most probably ovulating, when they'd made love?

She should have been going to bed with Chet. If she had been, she'd be on the Pill. Safe. But her sexual encounters had been limited to a one night rite of passage her senior year of college, and a week-long affair three years ago with a guy whose smile reminded her of River. So she hadn't ever stocked up on contraceptives.

Chet really should have pushed her more, tried to take her beyond kisses, a little experimental petting. But he hadn't, and she hadn't considered that a bad thing. To be honest, she still didn't consider that a bad thing.

More of a lucky escape, actually.

However, now she had done the most irresponsible thing imaginable. She'd had unprotected sex, in the middle of her cycle, with the one man who would hunt her down, force her to the altar, even if he hated the ground she walked on.

She stopped at the double glass doors and turned around to watch as River drove out of the parking lot, off to do some errands for Inez before picking her up again and returning her to the ranch.

Sighing, wishing her life less complicated, Sophie pulled open the door and walked inside...then walked outside an hour later, loaded down with papers explaining her home exercises, sore as hell, but minus her cane. Her knee was healed, they'd assured her of that in San Francisco before the J-brace came off for good, but her muscles had all gone soft, her calf muscle just about gone, and now she had entered the strengthening portion of her physical therapy.

Walking on the treadmill, five minutes on the stepper, time on the mat with John, her therapist, pushing and pulling on her leg, lifting it high, bending it toward her chest until she'd been drenched in perspiration.

She was tired, exhausted, and her leg throbbed like a toothache. She wanted the car, she wanted home, she wanted a long soak in a hot tub—but the SUV was not in sight.

"Damn it, Riv. I told you an hour. How hard could that be?" she muttered, looking around her, watching the traffic come and go at the shopping mall, as the rehabilitation center was attached to the outside of the mall as a convenience to those patients who had to use public transportation.

It was a shame there was no public transportation, running to the ranch, but that would be ridiculous. What was more ridiculous was that Sophie suddenly realized that she was standing with her back touching the brick wall, watching each passerby as if Jack or Jill the Ripper was in the mall crowd somewhere, looking for her.

"This is stupid," she told herself bracingly, then flinched as three long, lanky and faintly scruffy teenage boys strolled past, clad in shirts and jeans obviously designed for a circus clown on stilts but that had somehow ended up on these fashion dropouts.

The boy closest to her, old enough to try out a

patchy, rather pathetic goatee, turned and winked at her, saying, "Looking good, babe."

Sophie had to bite her lip to hold back her scream, fight down the urge to run back inside the rehab center and beg for help. Her skin had gone cold and clammy, her heart was pounding so hard in her chest that it actually hurt, and stupid, frightened tears burned behind her eyes.

Crazy. This was crazy. All right, so she hadn't been in public, alone, since the night of the mugging. But was that any reason to go all goofy and paranoid the first time she was out on her own? It was three o'clock in the afternoon, and she was anything but alone in the crowd of mall shoppers. It was daylight, she was safe, and she'd stand here and gut it out or know the reason why!

She deliberately squared her shoulders, stepped away from the brick wall and walked all the way across the wide sidewalk, to a pole support at the curb. Fighting the impulse to grab on to the pole for dear life, she leaned her shoulder against it as casually as possible and directed her attention to the main entrance to the mall some seventy-five yards away, watching mothers and babies, teenagers, seniors—all those safe, innocuous people—enter and leave the mall.

She was all right. She was safe. She could do this.

But when she felt a hand on her arm, she screamed, a short burst of panicked sound, and half jumped out of her skin.

"Whoa, Soph, what's the matter?" River said, letting go of her as he pulled her into his arms. "Are you okay?"

Sophie pulled away from him, gave him several quick whacks on the chest. "Don't you *ever* sneak up on me like that again, River James! Where *were* you? I've been waiting for hours!"

River cocked his head, looked down at his watch. "By my calculations, Ms. Colton, ma'am, I'm seven minutes late. My apologies." Then he used his thumb to tip back his hat, ran his green gaze over her. "You're scared spitless, aren't you, Soph? Look at you—you're pale, you're shaking. Why?"

"It's nothing. Nothing," Sophie told him, looking toward the parking lot, seeing the SUV with the words Hacienda del Alegria painted on the doors, and headed for it. "Just forget it, okay?"

"I don't think so," River told her once they were both in the front seat, strapping on their seat belts. "You were scared back there. Don't tell me this was the first time you've been out in public. You went to physical therapy in San Francisco, didn't you?"

Sophie was having trouble securing her seat belt, thanks to the tears blurring her vision. "Yes, I went to PT there, but I never went alone. Dad had hired a nurse. She was with me day and night until I came back to the ranch."

"Your nurse? Or was that your bodyguard?"

At last the belt snapped into place, and Sophie sat back, kept her eyes front, looking through the windshield, out over the parking lot. "She was my nurse, Riv. Don't read into things, look for stuff that isn't there."

"I wasn't," River pointed out, adding, "this one just sort of jumped up and bit me. You're afraid to go back into the world, aren't you, Sophie? Does Joe know? Have you considered talking to anyone about this?"

Sophie shot him a dangerous look, or at least it would have been, to anyone else. But not River. He had this maddening way of being oblivious to any warning that he might want to just shut up, mind his own business. "There's no need. Now, if you'd consider starting the car and getting out of here..."

"Yes, Ms. Colton, ma'am, anything you say, ma'am." River turned the key in the ignition, backed out of the parking spot, turned toward the exit to the highway as Sophie fiddled with the radio, hoping to fill the silence with music and avoid any more conversation.

"And stop calling me Ms. Colton ma'am," she said after a few minutes, because even the music coming from the oldies station couldn't stop River's voice from repeating and repeating inside her head. "It's silly."

"Yes, Ms.— Sorry about that," River responded, grinning at her. "I'm just trying to figure out where I fit in your life now, Soph. Not the older brother anymore, that's for sure, foster or otherwise. Not the hero in all your schoolgirl fantasies, definitely. You've just ruled out employee of the boss. So where does that leave us, Sophie? Besides counting down the days, I mean."

"I don't know," Sophie said, too upset to continue

verbally jousting with him. "I really don't know. Do you?"

He indicated the back seat with a slight nod of his head. "I was late because I couldn't decide which one to get, and ended up getting them all."

Sophie turned to look at the white plastic bag in the back seat, the one with the pharmacy name stamped on it in red ink. "What are you— Oh, God! You didn't!"

"Did you want to do it? I didn't think so, because it wasn't exactly easy for me. I think the girl behind the cash register was twelve. She blushed and giggled the whole time she was loading the bag."

Sophie bent her head into her hands. "I don't believe this. One time, River. One time. And it was my fault, so it's my responsibility. I goaded you into it, damn near double dared you."

"Yeah, my arm still hurts where you twisted it," River said, possibly trying for humor, but his voice had an edge to it that warned Sophie that he wasn't far from losing his temper. "You say *damn* a lot, Soph, in case you haven't noticed. Is that an advertising world word?"

"*Damn* is the advertising word for *golly-gosh-gee*," she told him with a toss of her head. "You don't want to know their word for *damn*. I just tried to keep up, striding the fence between goody-two-shoes and being outright vulgar. Besides, it fits. In every conversation with you, Riv, it fits." She looked back at the bag once more and shook her head. "Boy, does it fit."

"Damned because we did, damned if we know

what happens next, damned if you are and damned if you're not? Is that it, Sophie?'' River asked as he pulled into the passing lane, blew the doors off a semi rig hauling a slatted, wooden trailer filled with pigs.

''I'm just sorry it happened, that's all,'' Sophie said twisting her hands in her lap.

''I'm not,'' River told her, easing up on the gas as the turn into the ranch appeared over the crest of a slight hill. ''I hope you are pregnant. I want to marry you, Soph, and I'll take you any way I can get you.''

''Your timing stinks. Really, really stinks.'' Sophie turned her head away and closed her eyes. ''Go to hell, River James. You just go to hell.''

Sophie sat on a chaise longue in the courtyard near the pool, an ice bag on her right knee, watching the world grow dark and the stars come out. A quiet night, a safe hideaway, time to think—and the privacy to shed a tear or two.

Marry him? The man had the audacity to want her to marry him? How dare he!

And she'd thought the worst thing that could happen to her was to see pity in his eyes when he looked at her scarred face. Man, had she been wrong. This was worse, much worse. Now he wanted to marry her—*wanted* was definitely the wrong word—because she might be pregnant.

He had his honor. He had his duty.

He was lucky he didn't have a potted palm sticking out of his head!

And all without a word of love, either. Of course, that potted palm would already be growing through

his hat if he'd dared to use that word on her. At least
the man still retained *some* sense.

But, oh, how tempted she had been. That had been
the worst part—that she'd been tempted to take that
half loaf, say yes and close her eyes to the fact that
she was now an object of pity, a possible responsibility and a woman destined to be proposed to, first,
by Chet, for her money, and now because she was
such a pathetic loser.

"Are we having fun yet?" Sophie asked herself as
she sat forward and lifted the ice bag from her knee.

"Sophie? Are you talking to yourself? Hi, may I
join you?"

"Rebecca?" Sophie swung her legs over the edge
of the chaise and stood up, held out her arms. "Oh,
it's so good to see you!"

Rebecca Powell had been one of the many emo-
tionally challenged foster children taken in by Joe and
Meredith Colton over the years, and still lived nearby
now that she was past thirty and had been out on her
own for years. She was a teacher, working mostly
with those children with learning disabilities.

Tall and willowy, with the body of a dancer, Rebecca wore her long brown hair in a French braid,
had the kindest blue-gray eyes Sophie had ever seen,
and was, according to family gossip, the oldest living
virgin in California.

Rebecca returned Sophie's hug, then the two of
them sat down, holding hands for several moments as
they continued to look at each other.

"So?" Sophie said at last, as they grinned at each

other. "I know it's kind of dark out here, but what do you think?"

Rebecca's smile was slow and sweet. "I think I'm still six years older than you, and always will be. Will you still be so glad to see me when my hair starts turning gray? Or will that gray hair change your opinion of me?"

"You always did know just what to say, didn't you, Rebecca?" Sophie said, relaxing. "And I've got to stop this. It's like comments on this scar are a sort of litmus test I'm making everyone take before I can relax around them. I should have known better than to worry what you'd think."

"Maybe, but I should have done more thinking than I've done since hearing about your...your incident. Me, more than anyone else. But I didn't, and I want to apologize for that."

Sophie shook her head slowly. "What are you talking about?"

Rebecca shrugged her shoulders, sighed. "I was coming over tonight or tomorrow anyway, to welcome you home, figuring you should be allowed to deal with the multitude over the course of a few days, rather than all at once. We're a pretty intimidating bunch, taken all at once, right?"

"Right," Sophie agreed warily. "Go on."

"Yes, well, as I said, I was coming over anyway. But then River stopped by just as I was having dinner, and he told me you might be having a little problem..."

Sophie put her hands to her temples and pushed,

trying to keep her head from exploding. "He had no right—"

"Is he wrong, Sophie? Are you fine out there in the big bad world? Back to fighting form? Not looking at anyone and everyone as if they might just try to jump you, or knife you, or scare you back into your hideyhole? Can you trust, Sophie? How much confidence do you have in the good and the decency of your fellow man?"

Sophie swiped at her stinging eyes with the backs of her hands, sighed. "You know, don't you, Rebecca? You've been there."

"Been there, done that, have the scars and the T-shirt to prove it," Rebecca agreed. "And, unfortunately, even with all the therapists Meredith and Joe sicced on me, I'm not entirely over it yet. However, I'm better now than I was, better than I'd ever expected to be. I can function out there in the cold, cruel world, and can even see it as warm and kind again. You don't want to spend the rest of your life jumping at shadows, Sophie. Trust me on this. You've got to face your fears down, keep your chin up and don't let anyone or anything dictate how you live the rest of your life."

Sophie nodded, agreeing. "I think I hate that the most—that someone else has stripped me of my confidence, altered the way I look at life. Nobody should have that kind of power over us. Over our hearts, our minds, our reactions."

"So you're mad? That's good. As a matter of fact, it's probably half the battle. Get mad, stay mad, fight. Take back your life. Take back your independence.

Take back your right to walk the street, live your life without fear. Wiser, yes. More careful, definitely. But out there, Sophie. Don't let one man, one admittedly terrible incident, strip you of your freedom. He can't have that power over you, you can't let him have that sort of power over you. Get mad, cry, get it out of your system, and then move on.''

"He's dead, you know,'' Sophie said, sniffling, wiping her eyes once more. "Dad told me, tonight, after supper. He died of a drug overdose about a week after the attack, but nobody made the connection for a while. He's gone. He can't hurt me anymore.''

Rebecca reached out and squeezed Sophie's hands. "He never could hurt you, Sophie. Not in all the ways that count.''

"Hey, there you are!''

Sophie and Rebecca turned to see Emily and Liza approaching, the latter carrying a plastic bag from a local video rental store.

"We've come in search of any females with tear ducts,'' Liza said, waving the bag in front of her. "We rented three chick flicks, and with three you get free microwave popcorn. So, who's game?''

Rebecca looked at Sophie, who nodded her agreement.

"Why not?'' Sophie said, getting to her feet. "A good cry sounds like just what the doctor ordered. Right, Rebecca?''

"Sounds like a plan,'' Rebecca agreed, and the four of them headed back to the house, ready for a long evening of movies, of talk, and hopefully sprinkled with more than a few girlish giggles.

Just what the doctor ordered.

Eight

River used a fat marker to cross off yet another day on the calendar that hung on the wall just inside his office in the stables.

Ten days. Ten of the longest days and loneliest nights in his life.

He saw Sophie at the dinner table every night. But trying to hold a private conversation in the Colton household was about as impossible as spitting upwind in a tornado, and Sophie never appeared until the dinner gong rang, then took off again for her room the moment the meal was over.

Not that she was hiding in her room, becoming a recluse. On the contrary. She was always out. Rebecca picked her up some days and took her to the Hopechest Ranch, and Amber or Emily drove her into

Prosperino to shop, to visit the library—and to her physical therapy sessions.

River had been cut out of the picture, almost surgically removed.

He knew what she was doing. The question in his mind was why he was allowing her to do it.

Sophie walked out into the courtyard, then stopped, amazed to see her mother, dressed in her old gardening clothes, down on her hands and knees, pulling weeds.

The sight brought back so many memories of Meredith as she had been years ago. Loving the feel of the rich earth under her fingernails, swiping at an errant lock of hair that had fallen forward and carelessly smudging her cheek. Talking to her flowers, singing to them, babying them as she babied her children, loving them as she loved her children.

How long had it been since Sophie had seen Meredith pinching off dead blooms, planting new varieties of flowers she'd ordered from the dozens of nursery catalogs that arrived at the ranch with such regularity that Joe Colton had once asked his wife if she planned to bury them all in catalogs.

Years. It had been years.

Rather than disturb her mother, Sophie stood very still, watching as Meredith leaned closer to one of the copper tags that were pushed into the ground in front of every different type of flower, every shrub and small tree.

The tags had been Meredith's idea, and she'd expected all of her children to read them, learn as many

of the names as they could. Several varieties of tea
roses. Begonias. Brilliantly blue lobelia. Sea thrift and
dianthus and petunias. The tags held the more common, everyday names, and the Latin names as well,
as Meredith had always harbored the hope that at least
one of her children would take more than an ''Oh,
aren't they pretty colors!'' interest in gardening.

Her garden was one of the most startling disap-
pointments to the family, when Meredith abandoned
it after her accident, just as if she'd never cared about
flowers, about living things.

Living things, like her own husband, her own children, the children she had taken under her roof, into
her heart.

As far as Meredith was concerned, Sophie knew,
she had only two children. Joe Junior, who had shown
up on the Colton doorstep, a newborn, six months
before the automobile accident, and Teddy, who had
been born a year later.

Everyone else had just seemed to sort of disappear
from Meredith's line of sight, escape her interest.
Except for Emily, of course. Emily was ac-
tively shunned, detested, perhaps because Meredith
wouldn't have been in the accident at all if she hadn't
been driving Emily to a visit with her natural grandmother.

It wasn't rational. None of it was rational. The past
nine years hadn't been rational. So Sophie had fled,
stayed at college, visited friends during the summer
breaks, come home only for holidays then and ever
since. Unwilling to see River, who had rejected her,
unwilling to open herself to the rebuffs of her mother,

who had proved her disinterest yet again by not coming to San Francisco after the mugging.

And yet…and yet…

Sophie loved her mother. How could she not love her mother? Seeing her today, seeing her like this—dressed in old clothes, without regard of her manicure—watching her indulge in such a well-remembered domestic activity—well, it felt good to see it. It felt very, very good.

"Hi, Mom," Sophie said at last, walking over to where Meredith knelt, peering at one of the copper tags, this one stuck into the ground just in front of an oleander bush. Meredith had, in fact, just been reaching out with a small pruner to snip off one of the oleander branches as Sophie spoke.

"Wha-what!" Meredith exclaimed, jumping back slightly on her knees, dropping the pruner. She whirled around and glared up at Sophie. "You! How dare you sneak up on me like that?"

"Sneak up on— I didn't sneak up on you, Mom," Sophie said, all the sunlight having suddenly gone out of her day. "But I am sorry if I startled you."

"Should have kept the cane," Meredith muttered, rubbing her dirty hands together as she got to her feet. "At least I heard that coming. Well, what do you want? I know you didn't come out here just to frighten me. Or did you?"

Well, so much for a shared, idyllic moment among the posies. "No, Mom, I didn't come out here to frighten you. But I can help, since you taught me years ago how to tell the difference between a weed and a flower."

Meredith looked down at the small pile of uprooted plants lying on the patio stones. "Oh, them. I'm done now." She bent down, picked up a few sprays of oleander she'd cut from the bush and tucked them into the pocket of her slacks. "What dirty work! I need a bath."

Without another word, Meredith walked back to the French doors that led to her bedroom, leaving Sophie, and the pulled weeds, behind.

Sophie bent down to pick up the weeds, then went down onto one knee when she took a closer look at the wilted plants. Two petunias, one begonia, and two other uprooted plants she was pretty sure were sea drift. Meredith hadn't been pulling weeds—she'd been yanking out young plants, not yet budding flowers.

Why? Why would she do something like that? It was almost as if she'd not known what she'd been doing, hadn't recognized the plants, pulling whatever was closest, just to make it look as if she was busy. No. That was ridiculous, and Sophie banished the thought.

Looking at the oleander bush, Sophie traced her fingers over one of the bottom branches, able to see where the pruner had made fresh cuts in the younger growth.

Meredith had pulled, then left behind, flowers. She had trimmed oleander and taken it with her. It made no sense. It made no sense at all.

"Oh, Sophie?"

Sophie got to her feet, looked at her mother, who

had come back into the garden. "Yes? I was just cleaning up the...the weeds."

Meredith gave a dismissive wave of her hand. "Oh, that. Don't bother. It took me all of ten minutes to get bored with that. That's why we have a gardener, you know. Let him earn his keep."

Her mother was referring to Marco as a gardener? A simple employee? Inez and Marco had been at the ranch as long as anyone could remember, and they were more family than employees. Why, Meredith and Marco used to have a loving, running feud on Meredith's sometimes micro managing "his" gardens. The two of them often dug in the dirt side by side. Now Sophie just stared at her mother, unable to speak, to find an answer to the woman's callous statement. So she just nodded.

"Yes, well," Meredith said, looking down at her hands. "I've ruined my nails, haven't I? I suppose I'll have to go into town and have new tips put on. Oh, well. But, before I go, I wanted to tell you something, my dear. Something that will put a smile back on that sour puss of yours that you've been parading around in front of us all since you've been here."

Sophie wet her lips. "Oh? Really? What have you done, Mom?"

Meredith's smile was absolutely dazzling. "Why, I did what should have been done a long, long time ago. I've called and invited Chet Wallace to come up here for the weekend, or longer, if he wants. He should be here before dinner tonight, so I suggest you go...do something about yourself. Change your clothes—and for pity's sake, put some concealer over that scar. You look entirely too much like me for me to feel comfortable looking at you now.''

Sophie realized her mouth had dropped open, and closed it, but by the time she could even begin to form a reply to her mother, Meredith had turned on her heels once more, heading toward the French doors.

"Oh, God," Sophie whispered at last, all but staggering to a nearby chair and collapsing into it. Chet? Coming here? She didn't want to see him. She certainly didn't want River to see him.

River!

Sophie jumped to her feet, the uprooted flowers and trimmed oleander forgotten, and headed toward the stables.

River sat rump down in the dirt, his arms propped behind him, glaring up at the roan stallion. The damn horse was just standing there, reins dragging, looking as innocent as a six-week-old kitten. As he watched, the roan bared its huge teeth, lifted its head and gave a horsy laugh.

"Oh, so you think you're funny, do you?" River challenged, standing up, absently using his aged cowboy hat to beat the dust off his backside. "That's just because you don't know who's boss."

"Yes, he does!" Drake Colton called out from his perch on the top of the five-bar split rail fence. "And I've got a clue for you, River—it's not you."

River hid a smile, looked over at the navy SEAL, home on leave, and quipped, "Wise-ass. What are you doing here anyway? Don't you have to swallow a fish whole, or go balance a ball on your nose?''

Drake, both his coloring and his smile so like Sophie's, put his arms out straight in front of him and clapped his hands as he made seal-like noises, then shot back, "Did I ever tell you I know how to kill a man sixteen different ways with my bare hands?''

River grinned. "Yeah, but can you walk and chew gum at the same time?''

"Hey," Drake protested, "that's complicated. Just give me the easy stuff, like plowing through steamy jungles or setting up underwater explosives.''

"Right," River said, advancing toward the roan, who was pretending not to see him, even as the stallion started slowly backing up, prepared to make a break for it. "Now shut up and watch a master work, okay?''

"I kneel at your feet, oh master, to watch the miracle," Drake told him. "Shall I fetch the liniment?''

Smiling wryly, River held out his hand and slowly approached the roan. His voice low, soothing, he began talking to the horse, speaking to him in his Native American grandmother's tongue, telling the roan that he was magnificent, a truly splendid beast, and how much he, this lowly man, would be honored to be allowed on his back as they rode, rode like the wind, the roan's fleet hooves flying, all the power of his strong, pure heart and wild, brave spirit unleashed. Man and beast, as one, moving free across the land.

It wasn't the words, because the roan didn't understand the words. It was the sound of River's voice as he said those words, the look in his eye, the firm yet gentle touch of his hand against the stallion's sleek neck. It was the bond, an unspoken bond, that River felt with nature's creatures, that the horse recognized. He had nothing to fear from this man.

River kept talking as he slowly undid the cinch of the saddle, let it slide down to the dusty ground. He took off the bridle, removed the bit from the roan's tender mouth. "We don't need any of this, do we, boy? Just you and me, boy, just you and me."

There was a small sound from the direction of the fence, where Drake sat, and River spared a moment to look over, saw Sophie standing on the bottom rung, with her forearms braced on the top of the fence. She didn't say anything, because she knew better, but if he didn't stop looking into her eyes he would soon lose the rapport he'd gained with the stallion, lose his concentration.

"Pay no attention to the beautiful woman standing on the fence. Nobody's going to bother you, boy, I promise," River said, still reassuringly stroking the roan's coarse mane. "See? No more saddle. No more reins. Just you and me. We're just going to take a ride, if you let me. Just a small ride, around the corral. If you let me. Will you let me? Will you honor me with your trust?"

River took a deep breath, let it out slowly, and then, grabbing on to the roan's mane, his movements fluid, graceful, he half tugged, half leapt, until he was, within an instant, sitting on the stallion's bare back.

No bridle, no reins, no saddle. If the stallion bucked, as it had before, River would be tossed to the ground again.

River sat very still, waiting for the stallion to make up its mind—toss him off or accept him. And then, with one hand still tangled in the roan's mane, his body bent forward so that his mouth was near one pointed ear as he kept up his reassurances, his praise, River gently pressed his knees against the horse's flanks, urging him forward.

The roan, that had minutes earlier tossed River high in the air as it had bucked and kicked, walked around the corral on dainty feet, as if carrying a precious cargo.

River had the stallion slowly circle the corral three times, then dismounted, turned the roan over to one of his assistants, who could now easily slip the bridle back on and lead the horse away.

"Good job, buddy. You always were a show-off," Drake said as River approached the fence. River ignored him, looking straight at Sophie. Drake, who didn't become a navy SEAL by being unobservant, excused himself, saying something about having a job to do back up at the house.

"You haven't lost your touch," Sophie said as River climbed over the fence and jumped down in front of her. "That was very impressive."

"Actually, it was very stupid. I should have known he didn't want the bit. Not until he trusted me. But we'll be all right now, I think. His owner should be happy, once the two of them are reintroduced."

Sophie frowned. "He's not ours?"

"Nope. He belongs to a rancher on the other side of Prosperino. I'm doing him a favor. Something tells me his last owner was heavy handed with the bit, and

probably the quirt. He'd supposedly been broken to
the saddle but was still pretty much unridable when
Erik got him—dirt cheap, I might add. Now that he
trusts me, it'll just be a matter of getting him to ex-
tend that trust to Erik. He'll make a fine animal now,
a fine stud.''

"That's amazing. You're very good at what you
do. You always have been," Sophie said, turning
away from the fence. River followed her.

"What's up, Soph? Not that I'm not honored, but
what are you doing here? You've been avoiding me
as if I had the plague. I've been a real gentleman
about the whole thing, too, in case you haven't noticed. Although I will put you on notice now that I'm
not going to be such a gentleman for a whole hell of
a lot longer. So? Did you…have you…?''

Sophie bowed her head. "I don't know yet, okay?''
she said shortly, then shivered. "And you wonder
why I'm staying away from you? God, Riv, you're
driving me nuts! Am I? Aren't I? And whether I am
or I'm not, it's none of your damn business.''

"There we go with the *damn* again, if you'll excuse
me for pointing it out. As to the rest of the nonsense
you're spouting… Is that right? It's none of my business—my *damn* business? Did it all by yourself, did
you? I don't think so, Soph. But you know what? It
doesn't matter. It flat out doesn't matter. I want you.
You want me. That's obvious, and has been obvious
for a long time.''

She stopped walking and looked up at him. "Well,
no ego showing in that statement, Riv, is there? I want
you? Who says? You?''

River lifted his hat a fraction, settled it lower over his forehead. "You tell me, Sophie. If I were to take you in my arms and kiss you right now, kiss you long, and deep, run my hands over you, would you slap my face? Or would you kiss me back, hold me tight, moan low in your throat the way you did—"

The palm of her hand connected with his left cheek, and River stepped back a pace, lifted a hand to his stinging face and smiled. "Well, that was fun," he said, watching as Sophie seethed. "So, why are you here? Or do you just want to beat up on me some more?"

The hot color that had invaded Sophie's cheeks faded so quickly he nearly reached out for her, believing she might possibly faint. But then she spoke, and her words stopped him.

"It's Chet. Mom invited him for the weekend. He'll be here later tonight, probably before supper."

River turned half away from her, said something unlovely under his breath, then looked at her once more. "Meredith did this? Without consulting you? Why?"

Sophie lifted her arms, shrugged. "Why does she do anything she does? If we knew that, Riv, we'd have all the answers, wouldn't we?"

Meredith bent over the tiled counter in her bathroom, working the white marble pharmacists' pestle into the mortar, doing her best to reduce the oleander leaves into infinitesimal fragments, to liquefy them in a few drops of hot water.

She'd tried everything else to release their poison.

Soaking some of the flowers in hot water. Chopping the leaves as finely as possible, so that the pieces could be sprinkled on a salad, some other dish. She'd considered drying some of the leaves, because they might not have any smell or taste if she then dissolved them in liquid.

She looked down at the green mess she'd made, tears stinging her eyes. This wasn't working, wouldn't work. There was no way to get it into food, and no way putting any of it in a drink would go undetected.

Cursing under her breath, Meredith picked up the mortar and pestle, and angrily flung both against the wall, watching as they fell to the floor, the marble bowl breaking in two, wet bits of leaf sticking to the wall.

"Ah, well, there's still time," she said, mentally consigning the mess she'd made to whomever Joe Colton paid to clean it up—drones who did what they were told and didn't ask questions, didn't think any farther than their own noses.

She picked up the book she'd bought in Prosperino, then hidden in her room, turning pages as she walked out of the bathroom.

It was a lovely book, very handy, with hundreds of different poisons listed alphabetically. She sat down on the chaise longue in her sitting room, lifted her martini glass to her mouth, smiled at the stacks of creamy ivory envelopes holding the response cards for Joe's sixtieth birthday party. "Hmmm," she mused, turning her attention to the book once more. "Maybe mushrooms?"

Nine

River's attendance at the Colton dinner table had been hit or miss these past ten days, but he was present and accounted for tonight. He wore cowboy boots, freshly laundered jeans and a long-sleeved, snow-white cotton shirt with metal snaps as he stood in front of the fireplace, one arm draped over the mantel. He'd thrown a well-worn black leather vest over the shirt, and left his cowboy hat on one of the hooks inside the front door.

It was Friday night dinner, and there were enough Coltons at the ranch to make for a large dinner party in anyone else's home. Here, it was just another casual Friday night get-together, no big deal.

Rebecca had stopped over, and Liza had come back with her parents, her mother, Cynthia, and her father, Graham, Joe's younger and only brother. Jackson

Colton, Liza's older brother, was among the missing, but that was to be expected, and no great surprise. Jackson spent many of his days dealing with his father at the law firm connected with Colton Enterprises, and that was more than enough contact with his old man, as far as Jackson was concerned.

Amber, Joe and Meredith's youngest, was off somewhere for the weekend, with friends, but Emmett Fallon, Joe's buddy since his army days, and now one of the most important cogs in Colton Enterprises, had stopped in for drinks, along with his fourth wife, Doris. River had never liked Emmett. He didn't know why, and figured he didn't have to have a reason.

Emmett and Graham had their heads together as they poured themselves drinks, talking over some aspect of the business—as if they didn't get to do enough of that every day. The two men were quite different, with Graham holding on to his blond hair with a vengeance—and probably with the contents of a dye bottle—while Emmett, some years his senior, seemed to prefer the distinguished look of white hair, not that it was a good look for him.

They were both about the same height, under six feet, and with slight, slim builds. So unlike Joe Colton, who seemed to fill a room the moment he entered it. The biggest difference between Graham Colton and Emmett Fallon, however, was that Graham smiled a lot, and Emmett had perfected the petulant frown. If they were a comedy team, Graham would tell the jokes, and Emmett would be the straight man. Except they probably didn't tell jokes, at least not to each other. They were too deeply in competition with each other for that.

It was odd to see Emmett and Graham together, as it was no great secret that they felt they were in daily competition with each other for Joe's favor.

In their lifelong race to be Joe's most indispensable right arm, they'd both forgotten to hide the fact that, brother and friend, they both most sincerely hated Joe Colton's guts for being so successful.

Not that Joe knew that. River didn't even know that. Not for sure. But he sensed it, could almost smell the jealousy and ambition emanating from both men, and so he always watched, waiting, wondering if and when Joe Colton was going to figure out that his success had made enemies of his old friend and his only brother. Joe's kindness toward them, bringing them into the business, rewarding them for their connection to him, had served to make them both hate the ground he walked on.

All while they smiled to his face.

River would be more worried if Graham and Emmett disliked each other less, because then they could possibly form an alliance and do Joe some real damage. But Graham and Emmett distrusted and disliked each other, so much that they'd never be able to marshal the trust to go into cahoots and try to bring Joe down. That was the only reason either man still was able to chew steak with his own teeth—because, otherwise, River would have had it out with both of them long ago.

River smiled slightly as Graham's voice rose and Emmett's face turned florid. They were at it again—

two aging roosters who couldn't be in the same room for more than five minutes without starting to scratch and bite at each other. River pushed himself away from the mantel, losing interest in the bickering men, and watched as Sophie walked into the room.

She was dressed in a soft pink V-necked blouse and ankle-length flowered skirt that looked all wrong on her, even with a thick gold necklace around her throat. She wore flat-heeled shoes, because her recovering knee wasn't yet ready for high heels, but she still appeared stiffly formal rather than casual, and her pale cheeks and pinched mouth had her looking as if she'd just been summoned to the principal's office for a lecture.

Poor kid. She wanted to be here tonight about as much as she wanted to see a fly in the soup Inez would probably be serving shortly.

He walked over to her. "You're looking panic-stricken," he said, grinning at her because otherwise he'd gather her into his arms, tell her he'd protect her.

"Go away," she said succinctly.

"Why? So that you can stand here, your hands locked together so tightly that your knuckles are white, and wait for the doorbell to ring? Give me a quarter, and I'll answer the door, tell him you've moved to Australia."

She lifted her head, glared at him. "How do you know I'm not just dying to see him again?"

River reached up and scratched behind his ear. "Oh, hell, well in that case, I'll be off. Back to the fireplace, which has always had the best view of the room. This should be fun to watch."

"I hate you, River James. I loathe and detest you, and still can't figure out why I even told you that Chet was coming here for the weekend," Sophie said through gritted teeth. "And if you leave me standing here alone when he shows up, I'll never forgive you."

He laughed softly. "You know, Soph, I understand horses. I understand almost any animal out there, although I wouldn't want to try reasoning with an angry bear or anything like that. But I'll be damned if I'll ever understand women. Stay and you hate me, go and you hate me. How do I win?"

"You don't," Sophie told him, then grabbed at his arm as the doorbell chimed and Inez appeared out of nowhere, as she was so good at doing, and headed toward the front door. "Just stick close, and don't punch him anywhere, okay?"

"Can I trip him?"

"No, you cannot trip him," Sophie warned under her breath as Meredith floated into the room wrapped in emerald green silk and sailed by Sophie, leaving a wake of expensive scent River was pretty sure he could chew on. Sophie sighed. "Now what does she think she's doing?"

"Greeting her guest, I'd imagine," River said as Chet Wallace walked into the room, looking like an advertisement in *GQ*, and Meredith held out her arms to him, to give him a hug as she air-kissed him on both cheeks.

"So, can I safely assume we're having filet of fatted calf for dinner tonight?" River asked facetiously. "That's some welcome Meredith is giving the guy you booted out of your life. Maybe she didn't get the memo and doesn't know the engagement is broken?''

Sophie slanted him a look that could freeze salt-water. ''You're not helping, you know. Oh, God, here he comes. Riv, behave.''

It wasn't easy, but River did what Sophie had asked, stepping to one side as the three-piece suit, whiter-than-white-teeth and professionally styled hair advanced across the room and enveloped Sophie in a gentle hug, then kissed her cheek. ''Hello, darling,'' he said, keeping hold of her shoulders as he stepped back a pace, looked down at her face with enough concerned pity in his eyes to make River grind his teeth and wonder if Sophie might just hit the man herself and save him the trouble. ''How are you, sweetheart?''

River rolled his eyes at the asinine question, turning away. How was she? River could give old Chet a clue on that. She's wasn't happy to see her lover-boy, that's how she was. Or was this guy brain dead?

''I...I'm fine, Chet,'' Sophie answered, and River suppressed a groan. ''You're...you're looking well.''

''Looking well?'' Meredith scoffed, and River turned back to see Sophie's mother standing beside Chet, an arm around his waist. ''Chet, you're more handsome every time I see you. Sophie's such a lucky, lucky girl.''

''Thank you, Mrs. Colton,'' Chet said, not looking the least bit embarrassed by her gushing and hugging, or by the fact that Sophie was looking at him with about as much interest as she'd have in a three-days-dead fish.

River decided to have a little fun. "Wallace!" he exclaimed, stepping forward and shooting his right hand out so quickly that Chet flinched and involuntarily took a step back before reluctantly shaking River's hand. "Glad to see you could tear yourself away from the wacky world of advertising. Gonna be a great couple of days. We've got it all planned, you know. A full weekend of fun on the ranch. You do ride, don't you? I've got the sweetest roan stallion boarded here at our house of joy right now, just waiting for you. You can be up and ready by six tomorrow morning, right? Sophie and I like to get a head start on the day with our morning rides."

"Ride? I don't ride." Chet tried to get his hand back, but River wasn't letting go.

"You don't ride? Well, that's a kick in the head, isn't it? I was really looking forward to seeing you on that roan." River finally let go of Chet's hand, giving the guy a few points for not wincing at the bone-crushing grip he'd applied, and tried not to laugh as Sophie surreptitiously planted a sharp kick on his calf.

Joe Colton had entered the room and came up to them then, right hand extended, to welcome Chet. It was the first time in his memory that River had seen Joe looking like a plastic politician, with a plastic smile and a plastic "What a nice surprise. Good to see you, Chet," coming out of his mouth. Clearly Joe hadn't been in on the invitation, not that River had ever thought so, but it was just as clear that Meredith was delighted with Chet's presence, as well as Sophie's discomfort.

"I was just about to suggest that Chet and Sophie take a walk around the gardens before dinner, Joe," Meredith told him. "You know, get to know each other again?"

"Is that right?" Joe looked at his wife, his eyes hard. "How are you tonight, princess?" he then asked, turning to kiss Sophie's cheek. "You look a little tired. You had physical therapy today, didn't you? I know they're working you pretty hard. Maybe you should just sit down awhile and give your knee a rest? Come on, I'll walk you over to the couch."

It was a smooth move, and one Chet couldn't block. River grinned at him as Sophie and Joe crossed to the other side of the room. "Meredith?" River suggested, because he couldn't help himself. "Maybe you want to show Chet here around the gardens before it gets too dark," he suggested.

Meredith's eyelids narrowed as she glared at River. "I'm afraid not. I have to go tuck Teddy and Joe Junior in for the night," she said, twin flags of color flying high on her cheeks as she seemed to acknowledge that her husband and foster son had outmaneuvered her. "If you'll both excuse me?" she asked, then turned on her heel and flounced away.

"And then there were two," River said brightly. "I could introduce you all around, even if you have met everyone before, at Christmas. But, you know, I have an even better idea, Wallace. How about you and I take a walk outside and get to know each other better?"

"I know you just about as well as I want to know you, Mr. James," Chet told him, but he spoke as he was walking, because River had taken hold of his arm at the elbow and was leading him toward the French doors opening onto the courtyard. "Is this really necessary?" he asked, attempting to sound brusque, but coming off just a teeny bit whiny. "I could have pressed charges, you know."

"Coulda, woulda, shoulda," River sing-songed, opening the door and "helping" Chet through, onto the patio. "Keep moving, Wallace, to the other side of the fountain, out of sight of the family."

Chet did what he was told, probably because he'd been raised never to cause a scene. Or maybe he was just a lily-livered coward. River didn't much care why the man moved, as long as he did.

He did finally stop and take a stand on the far side of the fountain, saying, "Now look here, James. You don't like me. God knows you've made that plain enough. But Sophie loves me and I love her, and there's nothing you can do about that, understand? I'm here because Sophie asked me to come, and I won't leave unless she tells me to go."

River looked at Chet for long moments, then dropped his head slightly and looked at him some more, sizing him up, measuring him for the truth of his words. "*She* invited you?"

Chet finally looked away, breaking eye contact. "Yes, she did. Well, maybe not directly, but Mrs. Colton assured me that Sophie was miserable without me, needed me here."

River shook his head, laughed softly. "You're a real loser, aren't you, Wallace? Sophie sends you away and you stay away. Then Mama Colton tells you to show up and you come to heel like a well-trained lapdog. You know, those designer suits of yours hang on you pretty well, considering you don't have a spine.''

Chet actually took a step forward, his hands bunched into fists. ''Let me tell you something, James, I'm getting pretty sick of you,'' he said, rolling his shoulders. ''You sucker punched me once, but you won't do it twice. I was on the boxing team in college, I'll have you know. Not that I'm about to get into a fistfight with you, because I don't have a single damn thing to prove to you. I'm here for Sophie because I love her, and *you* can go to hell.''

River watched, one eyebrow raised, as Chet walked back into the house. ''Well, that's somewhat comforting,'' he told himself aloud. ''I was beginning to worry that Sophie had no taste at all. The guy's got at least a little bit of spine. It's not going to do him any good, but I'll give him points for not being a complete jerk.''

River was just stripping off his shirt when the door to his room over the stables opened, banging against the wall.

''How could you?'' Sophie demanded, catching the door on the backswing and slamming it against the wall one more time. ''Damn you, River James—how could you!''

''Evening, Sophie. Out a little late, aren't you? Has Chet gone to bed already? Guess maybe the long drive tired him out?'' River asked, continuing to undo the snaps on his shirt, and remove it, then carelessly toss it on a nearby chair.

She ignored his questions, clearly having her own agenda for this impromptu meeting. "You had no right. *No* right!"

"If you say so, Soph," he answered calmly, putting a hand to his belt buckle, but then deciding he'd probably already pushed her about as far as she could go for the moment. "But just so I'm sure we're both talking about the same thing, I had no right to do what?"

Her huge brown eyes, the ones that could melt like warmed chocolate, narrowed to slits as she walked straight up to him, rammed her index finger against his chest. "You know damn well what you had no right to do. Taking Chet outside, threatening him like some big bully cowboy," she told him, then sort of growled in exasperation. She dropped her hand to her side. "Oh, put your damn shirt on!"

River compromised. He picked up his black leather vest and slipped into it. "Better?" he asked, then hid a grin as Sophie's cheeks went hot and she turned away, refusing to look at him. "Gee, guess not."

Sophie shook herself, then turned to glare at him once more. "You're insufferable, do you know that? No, don't answer. Of course you know that. You work on it, don't you? You love to see me go crazy. You know just what buttons to push to make me go crazy."

"True, at least part of it," River agreed. "I didn't know about the vest, though, or I probably would have tried it sooner. You like it, huh?"

There wasn't any steam coming out of Sophie's nose or ears, but there could have been, she was that incensed. "I loathe you when you're like this, River James. Ever since I first saw you, you've been driving me crazy, teasing me, making fun of me, laughing at me. That's all I was to you, Riv, the gum on your shoe that you couldn't get rid of, so you finally decided to tolerate me—and now you're acting as if you own me."

River, who had been smiling, sobered. "That's not true, Soph, and you know it. You're the one who drove me crazy, remember? Tagging after me, not letting me perfect my angry young man routine, showing me that at least someone wanted to be around me."

"Yeah, well…" Sophie closed her mouth, shook her head. "Oh, forget it," she continued after a moment. "Just forget it. We had a good thing once, Riv. But not anymore. I'm not a kid and you're not obligated to ride to my rescue. Not over Chet, not for any reason. You got that?"

"Yeah, Soph, I got that," River said, but he was talking to the night air, because Sophie was already gone.

Ten

She slid her hands beneath the black leather vest, ran her fingers over his bare chest. Felt his warmth, felt his flesh ripple, tighten, at her touch.

She touched her lips to his skin, traced his nipple with the tip of her tongue, eased closer against him, sliding one hand down, down...to encounter the silver buckle of his belt.

Barriers. Always barriers.

Moaning low in her throat, she fumbled with the buckle, feeling frustration tangling with the passion heating her body, moving her head lower, to bite, nip, at his skin.

Brrrrinnng.

Sophie's eyes flew open and she jackknifed forward in her bed, her heart pounding, her throat dry, too dry to swallow. She glanced around the room, looked at the clock and slammed a hand on the thing to silence its insistent ringing, then fell back against the pillows.

"Oh, damn," she said, shakily raising a hand to her forehead, staring up at the ceiling that was striped with morning sun coming through the slatted wooden shudders at the window. "Damn, damn, *damn!*"

Sophie met Chet at the breakfast table, as he was already loading his plate from the buffet Inez always set out on the weekend. Inez was usually short-staffed on the weekend, Nora Hickman, her kitchen helper having time off. Chet had chosen three thin slices of cantaloupe, two fat strawberries, and was now neatly spooning yogurt onto his plate. A plain bagel with a stingy layer of reduced-fat cream cheese completed his breakfast.

"Good morning, darling," he said, showing himself to be as dense this morning as he'd been last night.

"Good morning, Chet," Sophie answered, busying herself by loading down her plate with a thick slice of ham, two spoonfuls of scrambled eggs, another of home fries, and topping it all off with a slice of cantaloupe, just because it was there. She could eat healthy, too, damn it. "I hope you slept well."

Chet put down his plate, then pulled back the chair next to him, waiting for Sophie to sit down. "To tell you the truth, I didn't. It's awfully quiet out here, isn't it? Next time I'll have to bring along a recording of street noises, just to make myself feel at home."

Sophie smiled, as she was supposed to do, then

reached for the carafe of coffee already on the table.
"I thought we'd take a drive this morning, Chet. We
need to talk."

He reached over, squeezed her hand. "We certainly
do. Besides, I have something for you, darling, something that belongs to you."

Sophie turned to him, searching for the right words,
but her father chose that moment to come into the
room, so she just smiled again, then lifted her cheek
for Joe's kiss.

"Beautiful morning, isn't it?" Joe asked, then
shook his head as Inez did another of her magical
appearances and began loading a plate for her em-
ployer. "Really, Inez, I wasn't going to cheat."

The housekeeper lifted the lid of a small silver
bowl and spooned out cholesterol-free eggs, then
placed three pieces of imitation bacon on the plate,
following up with two slices of wheat toast spread
with low-fat margarine. "Just be quiet," she scolded,
"and start on this. Your oatmeal is still in the kitchen.
And the yellow carafe has the decaffeinated coffee,
remember?"

Joe looked at his plate, then at Sophie, his expression comically pitiful. "The woman is killing me with
kindness," he said, then began poking at the too-
yellow eggs with his fork. "I live for Sundays now,
you know, because that's the only day she lets me
have the real stuff."

"You should try yogurt, sir," Chet said, his con-
descending tone scraping down Sophie's spine like
chalk on a blackboard. "Healthy, nutritious, and great
for the waistline. Plus, my total cholesterol is one-

eighty-six, with my LDL and HDL right in the middle of the normal ranges."

"Well, pin a medal on you," Joe Colton muttered as Chet got up, went back to the buffet table for more fruit, then excused himself and headed toward the kitchen, for Sophie had taken the last of the cantaloupe and he wanted to ask Inez for more.

Joe leaned across the table and whispered, "I can't believe you invited him up here."

Sophie leaned forward as well. "I didn't. Mom did. She only told me yesterday afternoon, when it was too late to head him off at the pass."

"Meredith?" Joe asked, his eyes going hard. "Well, why the hell did she do *that?*"

"You'd have to ask her, Dad," Sophie said, pushing her scrambled eggs around the plate with the tip of her fork. "I don't know what I'm going to do."

Her father looked at her for long moments. "What do you mean, you don't know what you're going to do? Do you want him back?"

Sophie shook her head, then turned her attention to her breakfast, as Chet was heading toward the table once more, his plate now loaded down with honeydew melon slices.

"Your housekeeper is a treasure, Mr. Colton," Chet said as he sat down. "And she certainly has your well-being very much in mind. Sophie, darling, you should think about your own diet, you know. It's never too late, or too early, to start eating healthy, thinking healthy."

Sophie bit her tongue—she'd nearly told him she was considering taking up smoking, just to see how he'd react—wondering if Chet had always been such a bore, or if she was so unhappy to see him that he couldn't please her no matter what he said or did.

She looked at him as he neatly cut the honeydew melon with knife and fork. Chet was in his usual weekend clothes: pleated dress slacks and silk, mock turtleneck pullover tucked into his waistband so that the Gucci buckle on his belt showed. He was tall and slim. Not exactly muscular, but without a spare ounce of fat on his body. His tasseled loafers always shone as if spit-polished, his hair was never out of place, and the gold watch on his left wrist had a black face, with a diamond marking twelve o'clock. His nails were buffed and neatly rounded, his cheeks freshly shaved, and the scent of Aramis clung to him.

Sophie tried to picture him in scuffed cowboy boots, faded jeans, a belt buckle designed by Levi Strauss, and a black leather vest slung carelessly over his bare chest.

Nope. It didn't work. Chet wasn't cut out for jeans or black leather vests. Not unless he was going to a Halloween party. Because, on Chet, it would be a costume. River, on the other hand, wore such clothes like a second skin, a skin he felt easy in, to walk a world he felt easy in, sure of himself, of who he was and what he wanted.

She closed her eyes, and saw River standing in front of her. The vest, the jeans, the cowboy boots. His long black hair below the brim of his cowboy hat—that was all that had been missing last night, the cowboy hat—his thumbs stuck through his belt loops, a slow, lazy smile on his face.

"Sophie? Sophie, are you listening?"

"Hmmm?" she said, her head snapping up as she realized her mind had been miles away, going places it had no business going, thinking thoughts it had no business thinking. "Oh, I'm sorry, Chet. I guess I'm not entirely awake yet."

Which was true, because part of her was stuck in her dreams...and very reluctant to let go.

"Apology accepted, darling," Chet said, and Sophie bit her lip to suppress a smile as her father made a rather rude noise low in his throat, then got up and carried his empty plate into the kitchen to exchange it for a bowl of oatmeal. "I thought we might drive into Prosperino today. Do a little shopping, stay there for dinner. How does that sound?"

It sounded about as exciting as watching paint dry, but Sophie just smiled and nodded and said something that probably sounded a lot happier than she felt. At least they wouldn't be alone all day, except in the car, and when she told him at dinner that she didn't want to see him anymore, well, Chet Wallace would never make a scene in public.

Louise Smith sat back on her haunches and smiled at her latest purchase, a small hydrangea plant with the most immense blue bloom topping it, rather like a colorful puff-ball on a stick.

Louise adored her garden, having turned nearly the entire small backyard of her house into beds devoted to tea roses, to perennials, to a long bed of cutting flowers. She'd had to consult books, not knowing the native plants in Mississippi, but she'd signed up for catalogs, checked gardening books out at the local library and, last year, finally got up the courage to join the local gardening club.

She got to her feet, swiped a stray lock of hair out of her eyes, unknowingly depositing a smudge of black potting soil on her cheek, and turned, looked at the rather large cardboard box sitting on the brick patio she'd built by herself the previous summer.

"What have I gotten myself into?" she asked, examining the box from all sides as she walked around it. "I think I may have bitten off more than I can chew this time, Sparrow," she told the brown tabby Persian just now sunning herself on a white wrought-iron chair.

The cat lifted its head, chirped at her and began washing herself with one fat paw. Sparrow talked, sometimes held entire conversations with Louise, but instead of a commonplace "meow," she sort of chirped in short bursts. Hence her name, Sparrow. At least that was Louise's explanation, the one she gave anyone who asked about the unusual name. Actually the name came to her during one of her dreams, which was too ridiculous to tell anyone.

Her entire life was ridiculous, begun nine years ago as far as her memory was concerned, but much more fully explained by a stack of official prison documents and doctors' notes that told of a past definitely worth forgetting.

"Well, enough of that," Louise told herself, picking up a large screwdriver and using it to rip open the tape holding the top of the box closed. She peeled back the cardboard bit by bit, feeling the effects of both the heat and her exertion, and finally stood back to look at the fountain she'd ordered from the local nursery.

All she had to do now was put it together in about six thousand easily followed steps written in hiero-glyphics, fill it with water, and plug it in to the nearest receptacle.

"And then I'll probably be qualified to single-handedly construct the next space shuttle," she grumbled, paging through the thick instruction booklet.

"Knock-knock. Anybody home back here?"

Louise smiled as she looked toward the garden gate and saw Dr. Martha Wilkes standing there, holding up a small picnic basket. "Oh, what a nice surprise. Come in, come in. I can use all the help I can get."

"Hi, Louise," Dr. Wilkes said, opening the gate, then depositing the wicker basket on a low table. She was dressed casually, in beige twill shorts and a simple V-necked shirt with a leopard-skin pattern, her hair tucked beneath a triangle of bright orange cotton.

"Wow, is that the fountain?" she asked, walking around the box, shaking her head at all the pieces. "After you told me it was being delivered today, I decided that, since it's Saturday, maybe I'd stop by and lend a hand. I'd say you could use more than one hand. I hope you're good at jigsaw puzzles."

"I should have paid extra for assembly and setup, shouldn't I?" Louise said, shaking her head. "But I've always loved a challenge."

"Really?" Dr. Wilkes said, tipping her head as she looked at her patient and friend. "Well, so do I. What do you say we get started?"

* * *

River watched as Erik Tapler guided the roan stallion around the corral, occasionally flashing River a wide grin. After three hours of education and getting to know each other, horse and rider were doing just fine, and River felt a small surge of satisfaction knowing that he'd had a hand in bringing man and beast together.

Besides, it gave River something to do besides walking around the stables, muttering a lot and kicking things while he waited for Chet Wallace's BMW to come back up the road leading to the house.

"I can't believe it," Erik said as he dismounted, patted the roan's neck. "He's a new horse. You're a miracle worker, River. What do I owe you?"

River lightly jumped down from the five-barred gate and went over to stroke the stallion's velvety nose. "One free stud service ought to do it."

"For you, or for Colton Enterprises?" Erik asked as he removed the saddle and handed it to one of the Colton stable hands before leading the roan toward the horse trailer just outside the gate.

"For me," River said, following after his friend. "How did you know?"

"Well, I heard something about it somewhere. Joe Colton gave you some land and you're going to be building your own stud as well as running his. Do I have that right?"

"Almost right, Erik," River told him, amazed at how fast news traveled. "I've *bought* some ranch land from Joe, and am now mortgaged straight up to my neck, as I'm planning a good-size stable on the property, and my own house. Joe's holding the paper, which was his idea, but he knows I'll pay him back. Every penny."

"Anybody who knows you knows that, Riv," Erik agreed, nodding his head. "Wow. Running this stable, building your own. You're going to be a busy man."

"Sometimes that's a good thing," River said, watching the empty road. "Besides, it's time I started thinking about making my own fortune. You can't be around the Coltons for long without thinking about your own fortune."

The roan was led into the trailer without a problem, causing Erik to shake his head. "It took five of us to load him to bring him over here. I tell you, Riv, you'll be a millionaire in a week, with that talent of yours." He held out his hand, and River shook it. "Well, good luck to you, not that you'll need it."

"Thanks, I'll take it." River stood in the middle of the gravel drive, watching truck and horse trailer drive off, then sighed, turned back to the stables, pretty sure the BMW wouldn't be arriving back at the ranch until after the sun had been down for hours.

Luck? Hell, he'd take all the luck he could get.

Chet could still be an entertaining companion, a fact that rather amazed Sophie as they walked around Prosperino, peeking into shops, stopping for ice cream, sitting in the park for an hour, watching the world go by.

Chet was bright, sometimes funny, and with a

seemingly endless store of anecdotes, about his clients, about the world in general.

But, then, Chet was a salesman. He'd certainly sold himself to Sophie.

But it was all froth, and Sophie realized that now. Chet was all surface. He had his good looks, his impeccable wardrobe, his nice manners. He had his collection of stories, his "trust me" grin, and some pretty smooth moves.

If she wanted to sell toothpaste, she'd plunk down the bucks to have Chet Wallace plan the advertising campaign. No question.

But that didn't mean she wanted to marry the guy.

She should have realized it sooner, much sooner. But Chet had decided to sell himself to her, and he'd done a good job. He'd sold himself, and his ideas for the future—his future—all before she could look deeply enough to realize that there *was* no "deeper" to Chet.

Now they sat across the table from each other in a small dimly lit restaurant, and Chet was doing it again. Selling himself.

"I can't tell you how sorry I am that I let you walk home that night, Sophie," he was telling her earnestly, reaching out to take her hand. "I've kicked myself all around the block, several times, for that one."

"It wasn't your fault, Chet," Sophie told him, thankful to remove her hand as the waiter placed shrimp cocktail in front of Chet, a cup of soup at her place. "I was angry, and I left. And I didn't pay attention to my surroundings as I walked, which was also my fault. So let's just drop it, okay?''

"But I want to make it up to you,'' he persisted. He reached into his slacks pocket and pulled out a piece of white paper he'd folded into quarters. Unfolding it, he said, ''Here. Look. I've made up a new logo.''

Sophie turned her head slightly and looked at him out of the corners of her eye. ''You've made up a *what?*''

''A new logo, for our company,'' Chet explained, unfolding the paper. ''You know, I've decided that, business-wise, it would be smart to keep your maiden name. Colton. I mean, it's the gold standard when it comes to dependable, reliable, all that good stuff. So, instead of Wallace and Wallace, I figure we should go with Colton and Wallace. C & W. Look,'' he said, holding out the paper. ''See how I've entwined the two letters? What do you think of the font?''

Sophie felt her stomach clamping, effectively robbing her of her appetite while at the same time making her feel as if she'd been punched in the gut. ''Chet,'' she said earnestly, searching for a way to say what had to be said. ''Chet, it...well, this isn't going to work.''

He looked down at the paper and frowned. ''Really? Wrong font? I guess it could be less modern. I know you like traditional print. Okay, back to the drawing board.''

''No, Chet, not back to the drawing board,'' Sophie told him, pushing her untouched cup of soup to one side. ''I...I'm getting out of the business. That's what

I was trying to tell you that night. I wasn't all that sure then, but I am now, having been away from it all these weeks. It's not what I want, what I set out to do with my life. I don't think I could face going back to that world."

"Oh, okay. I understand now." Chet's look was part concern, part shock and—amazingly—part "poor, misguided girl." He took a deep breath, sighed. "It's the scar, isn't it? Pretty wicked, I agree. But you wouldn't have to see clients, Sophie. I could handle that part. Actually, until you can get it fixed, or use some sort of stage makeup to cover it up, that's probably for the best."

Sophie sat back in her chair, unable to speak, which didn't stop Chet, who barely took a breath before reaching into his pocket again, pulling out a small black velvet box she recognized with a sinking heart. "Chet...no," she said, sighing.

Finally—*finally*—the penny dropped, and Chet figured out that Sophie wasn't jumping at the chance to make up, make it all better, put his ring back on her finger.

"Sophie?" he asked, frowning. "What's wrong? Your mother said—"

"Ah, yes. My mother," Sophie replied sadly. "Tell me, Chet. What did my mother say?"

Dr. Wilkes sat back on the chair and smiled as Louise plugged in the fountain, then switched it on. "Ah, perfect! And it only took us—" she raised her arm, looked at her watch "—six months."

Louise stood up, pressed her hands to the small of

her back as she stretched. "Very funny. But it does look nice, doesn't it?"

Dr. Wilkes nodded, smiling. "It looks fabulous, Louise. And I love the sound of it, don't you? Louise? Don't you love the sound of it?"

Louise was standing unnaturally still, her face suddenly quite pale, her full bottom lip trembling as she stared at the fountain.

"Louise, what is it?" Dr. Wilkes asked, coming over to put an arm around her friend. "What's wrong?"

"I...I..." Louise shook her head, as if trying to snap out of a trance. She pressed a hand to her mouth for a few moments, then took a deep breath, blinked several times as if to keep back tears. "I don't know. It's brand-new, and yet I've known it forever. Heard it forever." She stabbed her hands into her hair, covering her ears. "Turn it off, Dr. Wilkes. Please... please turn it off."

Dr. Wilkes did as Louise asked, then came back to her patient, gently prying Louise's hands away from her ears, holding her cold fingers within her own strong hands. "Louise, look at me. Tell me what you remember. Tell me what you feel."

Louise wet her dry lips, slowly shook her head, her eyes directed at the doctor, but obviously not seeing her. "There are flowers. Flowers everywhere. The smell of the ocean. Sky. So much blue sky, wide and high, with cotton candy clouds. Do you see me? I'm there. I can see me. I'm on my knees, pushing something into the ground. A marker. Yes, some sort of small metal marker, with writing on it."

She blinked, then looked at Martha Wilkes. "Oleander. It's oleander. *Nerium oleander.* Such beautiful, deep green leaves. An evergreen, you know, with lovely flowers. Red. White. I like the pink best. I keep the children away, though, because it's pretty, but really quite poisonous. The leaves, the flowers, even the wood." She smiled, her face suffused with joy and love. "Not, as I told him, that I expect the children to gnaw on the branches."

Dr. Wilkes blinked back tears of her own as Louise's eyes cleared for a moment, then filled with panic as all the blood drained out of her face. "Louise? Are you all right?"

"No...no, I'm not," Louise whispered, closing her eyes, swaying where she stood. "Oh, God, I'm going insane, Dr. Wilkes, aren't I?"

"No, Louise, you're not. I promise you, you're not going insane."

"Then what is it? What's going on inside my head?"

Dr. Wilkes led Louise to a chair, her patient responding much like a doll that could be placed just where you wanted it, then stay there until you wanted it again. "I'm not sure. But we're going to find out, Louise. I promise you. We're going to find out."

Eleven

———

Sophie stood in the drive in front of the house, watching as the BMW's taillights disappeared into the darkness.

It had been a long day, and Chet probably should have stayed the night, but she couldn't deny that she was glad he'd chosen to start back to the city, stopping at a motel along the way if he got too tired. And he would, too. Chet was very safety oriented—at least when it came to his own safety.

"And his total cholesterol is a very laudable one hundred and eighty-six," Sophie reminded herself, at last able to smile as she remembered the exchange between Chet and her father that morning.

Her smile faded, however, as she turned back to the house. Was her mother still awake? Should she wait until the morning before seeking her out? Could she hope to get any sleep if she didn't talk to her tonight?

No. Probably not.

Squaring her shoulders, Sophie headed toward her mother's bedroom, not sure if she was glad or dismayed to see a light still burning under Meredith's door.

She knocked, tentatively, and then pushed open the door, stepped inside the large room. The bed had been turned down, but was empty. She glanced toward the sitting room that branched off from the main bedroom. "Mom? Mother? Are you in here?"

That was strange. Where was she, if the lights were on, and she wasn't in bed or stretched out on the chaise in the sitting room? Sophie looked toward the bathroom, but the door was open, the interior of the large room dark.

Sophie walked further into the room. "Mom? Hey, Mom? It's me—Sophie."

There was a small sound coming from behind her, inside the sitting room, a pathetic and only possibly human sound. She'd only peered through the closed, glass-paned French doors that separated the sitting room from the bedroom and not opened them.

Now she decided to take a closer look.

"Mom?" she repeated, opening one of the doors, tiptoeing inside the feminine hideaway furnished to look like a display in a home and garden magazine. She moved to her left and turned on the nearest lamp.

"Mom!" she exclaimed as Meredith, who crouched in the corner beside the French doors, her knees drawn up to her chest, lifted her crossed hands to her eyes and whimpered. Sophie rushed to her side, went down on her knees. "Oh, my God! Mom! What's the matter? Are you sick? Did you fall?"

"Go away, go away," Meredith implored pitifully, burying her face in her hands. "You hate me. I know you hate me. Go away."

Sophie didn't know what to do, what to say. Her mother had been in here, in the dark, crouching in the corner like a frightened child? It didn't make sense. "Hate you? Mom, don't be ridiculous. Just stay right here. I'll go get Dad," she said, trying to rise, but Meredith's hand snaked out to grab her, hold her still.

"No! Don't go, Sophie. Don't leave me! Oh, why can't I do anything right? I brought Chet here for you, and you sent him away. Oh, yes, Sophie. I saw him, you know, talked to him. He told me I should have minded my own business. He hates me, too. *Everybody* hates me. I do everything wrong. I just want to sit here in the dark, be alone, and have a good cry. I'm such a mess."

Sophie's brain was reeling. How could her mother react like this? Overreact like this? "Mom, it's okay. Really. Chet and I had already pretty much known that our engagement wasn't going to work. We're still friends, honest, and I'm going to be his silent partner in his new agency, because he's very good at what he does. So he's fine. He's happy as a clam, now that I think about it."

Meredith narrowed her eyes, suddenly looking quite fierce. "He took your money? My God, of course he did! They're all alike, all of them! Take and take and take. My little Jewel, taken. My life, taken. Everything gone…'' Meredith's words trailed off and she slowly got to her feet, nearly tripping over the long, flowing silk caftan as she pushed past Sophie and headed for the bathroom.

Sophie followed her, watching from the doorway as her mother opened a drawer next to the sink and pulled out a small brown plastic medicine bottle. Meredith tapped two large blue pills from the bottle, threw them into her mouth, swallowed them dry, then pressed her palms against the counter and smiled at her reflection in the mirror. ''There. That's better.''

Sophie walked into the bathroom, one hand held out. ''Let me see that bottle, Mom. What are you taking? Who prescribed it for you?''

Meredith's mood seemed to shift yet again, and she smiled. ''I'm seeing a doctor in Prosperino, and he says I'll be fine, if I just take these pills. Just a little problem with my nerves, left over from…from the accident. And then the separation between your father and me, then having another baby, and going through menopause these past few years. Well, it has been hard, Sophie, so very hard. Hard on me, hard on your father, hard on all of us. And I'm sorry, Sophie. I'm so, so sorry.''

''I know, Mom, I know,'' Sophie soothed, hurting for her mother while at the same time rejoicing inside that, at last, her mother was opening up, talking to her.

''I was doing much better, until you were hurt, and then I lost ground. That's why I didn't come to you, Sophie, because I felt so sick. You understand that, don't you? But we can't tell your father, especially since I'm already feeling better, now that you're home with your father and me again. No, we can't tell your father. Not with his condition. You know how depressed he is, Sophie. We can't burden him anymore, now can we? Promise me, Sophie. Promise me this will be our little secret. Because I feel much better now, I really do.''

"Mom—"

"No, no, really," Meredith persisted, seeming to slowly take control of herself once more. "We're going to have a party, Sophie. A great big party to celebrate your father's sixtieth birthday. And then we're going on a cruise. Oh! Don't tell him that. That's a secret, my birthday present to him. My...my doctor says it will do us both a world of good. So you see?'' she ended, taking in a deep breath through her nose, letting it out slowly. "You see how it would ruin everything if you talked to your father? I'm doing better every day, I really am. Tonight was...just a small setback, that's all.''

She leaned over, kissed Sophie's cheek and hugged her. "See? I'm fine now. Everything's fine now. And I'm so sorry, Sophie. My own dear little girl. I'm so very sorry for screaming at you like that. Please, forgive me.''

How long had it been since Sophie had felt her mother's arms around her? Too long. She returned her mother's embrace, willing to forget anything, all the harsh words, all the strange statements, if only her mother would hold her, stroke her hair, love her. She held Meredith, and she sobbed.

"Okay, Mom," Sophie said at last, sighing,

breathing in the scent of her mother's perfume. "It'll be our secret. At least for now, it will be our secret."

River hastily stood up as he saw a dark shape revealing itself against the even darker background of the night.

He'd been sitting on the bench outside the stable, feeling fairly good about the world in general ever since he'd seen Chet Wallace's fancy sports car heading away from the ranch an hour earlier.

It may have been petty, to take joy in old Chet's obviously early departure, but he'd take his jollies where he could get them.

But now he wondered—somewhat belatedly, he realized—why he hadn't thought too much about how Chet's departure would have affected Sophie. Was she relieved? Feeling guilty?

River watched as Sophie came closer, knowing her slight limp even in the dark. "Over here," he said, stepping out of the shadows, into the soft yellow light of the pole lamps. "What's up, Soph? You didn't have to walk all the way down here in the dark. If you'd phoned, I'd have come on up and— Hey, what the hell?"

Sophie had run the last few steps toward him, and now was plastered against him knee to chest, holding on to him for dear life, sobbing on his shoulder.

"Soph, calm down, sweetheart," he said, returning her hug, rubbing at her back, his heart sore as he felt her tremble against him in her grief. "What's wrong? Did he hurt you?" The thought had him grabbing Sophie's shoulders, pushing her slightly away from him so that he could peer into her face. "Sophie, for God's sake, answer me! Did he hurt you?"

She shook her head, almost violently, then grabbed at him once more. "Hold me, Riv. Please, just hold me."

So he held her. There wasn't a whole hell of a lot else he could do. He waited for the storm to subside, then finally reached into his pocket for a blue-and-white folded handkerchief, handing it to her, waiting until she'd wiped her eyes and blown her nose.

"You can keep it," he said at last, trying for a little humor, just to break the tension. "In fact, if you're going to keep this up, I'm going to buy you a gross of the things for Christmas."

Sophie gave out with a short, self-deprecating laugh, then reached up to stroke River's cheek. "I'm sorry, Riv. I've got to stop doing this. Dumping on you. But...but it's been one hell of a day."

"Wallace?"

She looked at him, her expression puzzled for a moment, as if she'd forgotten the man existed. "Chet? Oh, no. Chet didn't do anything. He was more than happy to take my money and run."

River tipped his cowboy hat back on his head, looked at her quizzically. "Your money? What did you have to do, Soph, pay him off?"

That got another small smile out of her. "No, I did not, you idiot. But he did finally understand the benefits to be had in being my business partner rather than my fiancé. I'm to be his silent partner, by the way, which also works for both of us. He's probably already halfway back to the city, crunching numbers in his head, planning a new logo for his agency. Probably something with a very modern, avant-garde font.''

"Logo? Font? You know, Sophie, nobody would blame me if I slapped your face, thinking you were more than a little hysterical.''

At that, Sophie's smile faded, and she gave a small shiver, as if a cold wind had just blown across her shoulders. "Can we talk?'' she asked after a moment, her liquid brown eyes pleading with him. "I—I really need to talk to you.''

He led her toward the bench, then changed directions, taking her hand, leading her around to the outside stairs that ran up to his small rooms above the stable. He preferred living here, near his horses, rather than in the main house with the family, where his room sat unused.

Once he got her settled in the living room, he grabbed a beer out of the refrigerator for himself and poured her a glass of white wine—the wine he'd bought the day before she came home, in the hope that one day she'd be here with him.

She took the glass, sipped at its contents, then put it down on the small coffee table as he sat down beside her on the couch. "Thanks. I guess I needed that.''

"Yes, I guess you did, too. Now I'm wondering *why* you needed that.''

She told him. He sat very still, watching her closely, as she told him.

"You should have gone with your first instincts, gotten Joe,'' he said at last, as Sophie wiped at her moist eyes yet again. "He needs to know this, Soph. This is beyond you, beyond me."

She shook her head. "I promised, Riv. I promised it would be our secret."

"Then you came here and told me," River pointed out, swallowing down the last of his beer. It tasted bitter, and he didn't think he'd want another one.

"Yes, I did, didn't I?" Sophie said, sighing. "And now you're in on the same promise, the same secret. You won't tell my dad, will you?"

He wanted to. Oh, God, how he wanted to. "No, Soph. I won't tell him. Besides, I'm pretty sure he already knows. Aren't you?"

She bit her lips together, then nodded. "Yes, I suppose he does. She...she's got problems. Big problems. I mean, her mood just shifts from happy, to sad, to boiling angry. It was like watching a chameleon change colors in front of my eyes. She loves Dad, I'm sure of that. And yet...sometimes I think she hates him, hates everybody. And she's afraid of him, afraid of all of us. We're cluttering up her life, we're in her way, we're making demands on her she can't handle. All she wants is to be left alone, just her, and Joe Junior, and Teddy. It's as if nobody else matters. Oh, she's planning this big party for Dad, but that's just because she thinks she has to, I can tell. I don't think her heart is in it."

River lifted one eyebrow. "Really? I think you're wrong there, Soph. Meredith does like her parties, the bigger and showier the better. You can't deny that."

Sophie took another sip of her wine. "I guess you're right. There have been a lot of them over the past few years, haven't there? And none of them any fun.''

''Not for you maybe, but Meredith has a whole scrapbook stuffed full of photographs and stories clipped from the Prosperino newspaper and others. I saw it one time. She's got everything in there, and has drawn hearts and stars on the pages, little arrows pointing to each picture of her, each mention of her name.''

''I didn't know that,'' Sophie said quietly. ''That's sort of sick, too, isn't it? Well, not sick, exactly. But juvenile. Damn, Riv, why is she acting this way? When she opened up to me, when she held me— Oh, Riv, it was so good to have her hold me again, the way she did when I was little. But now, now that I'm away from her, I keep remembering how she looked. Heartbroken, then wild-eyed, and then almost too happy. If I've seen all this, what has Dad been seeing? He's so protective of her. He must know, mustn't he? He must know even more than we do.''

River took the glass from Sophie's hand, placed it on the table as he turned toward her. ''Let's not talk about this any more tonight, okay? It will only upset you.''

Sophie stood up abruptly, skirted the coffee table, and began pacing on the area rug that River had bought on his last trip to the reservation.

''Well, of course it upsets me, River,'' she said angrily, her arms waving as she all but stomped up and down the rug. ''Wouldn't you be upset? My mother is falling apart. My father walks around looking like he just lost his last friend, and has pretty much cut himself off from the business. Rand tells me that Peter McGrath and my cousin Jackson are just about running the corporation, and keeping tabs on Uncle Graham and Emmett Fallon, because both of them would rob Dad blind if they could. His brother and his best friend—ungrateful bastards, the both of them, watching him like vultures, ready to come in to pick his bones.''

"We're all watching them, Sophie. Nothing is going to happen there, I promise.''

"But we shouldn't *have* to worry about it! None of this should be happening. Amber stays away from home as much as she can, Emily still blames herself for the accident that seems to have triggered all of this, and Drake says he feels less tense wiring underwater explosives to the bottom of a ship than he does at our own dinner table. I don't remember the last time we've all been together just because we want to be together—Rand, Drake, Amber, Chance and Tripp and Rebecca, Emily, Wyatt, Blake. We used to be here all the time, all of us, and now we're scattered, hiding. It isn't just that we've all grown up, gotten started on our own lives. It's that there's nothing here for us anymore, and we all know it. We're all going to hell in a handbasket, Riv, the whole damn family— and I don't know what I can do about it.''

"And that's the crux of it, Soph. You *can't* do anything about it. None of us can. Joe says you have to take the good with the bad, and that's just about all we can do, at least until Joe finally figures out that his wife is gone, and we're all living with nothing more than a shell of the woman we all knew and loved.''

Sophie stopped pacing, wrapped her arms around herself. "That's so cold, Riv. It's like we've all given up, even as we pretend to keep fighting, keep hoping. Mom said tonight that we'd taken her jewel away. You know what I think she meant? I think she meant her life. As if Dad, all of us, have taken her life away. The bright, shining jewel that was her life. Bit by bit, we dragged her down. All us kids, all the kids that grew up here. Dad going to Washington, leaving her here with all of us. Michael's death. The accident with Emily. The separation before Teddy was born. It's been too much for her, we asked too much of her.''

"So you're going to keep silent about what happened tonight?'' River asked, coming around the table, to put his hands on her shoulders. "Do you really think you're doing her a favor keeping that sort of secret?''

"I don't know, Riv. I don't know anything anymore,'' Sophie said, pressing her cheek against his chest. "I just know I don't want to go back up that hill tonight, be in that house. That sad, sad house.''

River bent his head, nuzzled his mouth against her throat. "Then stay here, stay here with me.''

Twelve

This was wrong, so wrong.

And so right.

Sophie felt herself being lifted high in River's arms, and she didn't protest. It was difficult to protest when she had her mouth locked with his, her fingers convulsively digging deep into his thick hair.

She felt herself going down, gently down, her back against the soft quilt. River was still with her, as her arms wrapped around him, unable, unwilling, to let him go.

This wasn't love. This was need. This was release, the wild, panicked longing for a blessed deliverance from tension, the cessation of a devastating emotional pain. This was wanting…wanting to be held, wanting to feel desirable, wanting all the nightmares gone. That's what she needed. She needed all of it gone, all of it shattered by River's touch, River's kiss, his hands on her, his strength all around her, protecting her.

There was also a hunger deep inside Sophie, a hunger she'd never allowed to surface, not to this extent. She longed to devour, to be devoured.

River's hands skimmed her, tracing small paths of fire on her skin, and she clawed her fingernails down his back, trying to reach him through his shirt. Hunger.

His tongue delved deeply into her mouth and she felt her teeth scrape against his as she dueled with him, dared him, battled for dominance, took what she wanted, what she needed so desperately.

Their clothes disappeared, not without damage, but that didn't matter. Clothes were replaceable, a nuisance, and only served as an impediment to desire. If she had her way, the two of them would be naked for the next fifty years, or at least for the next few minutes. Minutes, seconds, fleeting moments…heartbeats racing time, speeding time, destroying time in order to hold the moment, keep the moment.

Sophie moaned with loss as River's mouth left hers. But then he was at her breast, teasing, licking, nipping. "Yes," she whispered hoarsely, her head thrown back, her eyes tightly shut in case reality dared to look at her, dared to destroy the moment with even a small hint of sanity. "Yes, River…please."

Something hot and wild coiled deep in her belly, tugged into life as River suckled at her, shaped her, molded her into anything he wanted. Anything he needed. She'd give it all to him, anything, just as long as he didn't stop. *Please don't stop.*

Her mind spiraled out of control as River kissed her. Kissed her flat belly, her hip, some sweet, unreachable spot behind her knee.

Make me forget, she pleaded inside her head. *I don't want to hurt anymore. I don't want to be afraid. Help me, River. Help me forget. Love me...love me.*

River woke slowly, wincing as he moved, feeling as if he'd spent a week in the saddle, his every muscle sore, depleted and yet strangely liquid, satisfied.

He felt Sophie's heat next to him as they'd fallen asleep together, the curve of her back against his belly. He still had both arms around her, one under her, the other protectively draped around her waist.

He moved forward slightly, dipping his face into her hair. She smelled so good. Wildflowers. A woman gone wild. A woman who had given until she couldn't give any more, a woman who had taken all he had, then taken even more.

And never a word of love.

River winced as he slowly withdrew his arm from beneath her, not at the pain in his tensed muscles, but with the knowledge that last night had proven nothing—except that they were two healthy animals with strong passions, strong desires.

Worse, she was going to hate him when she woke up, finally came out of the dream and realized what she had done, all that she had allowed, welcomed.

Because she'd come to him out of pain, out of despair, and he'd used her heartache, taken her to his bed, let her kiss and bite and claw her way through the pain.

Their first explosion of passion had rocked them both, and she'd looked horrified when it was over. She'd tried to leave him, to run away yet again.

But he hadn't let her do that. He couldn't let her do that.

So he'd gentled her, talked to her, stroked her, soothed her, using all his skills, all his experience in calming frightened, spirited but hurt animals. Gaining her trust, at least for a little while, then loving her again, slowly, gently, until she'd melted in his arms, wept in his arms, finally slept in his arms.

But she'd hate him this morning. If he knew nothing else about Sophie, he knew that she'd hate him this morning, because he had seen her vulnerable, broken. She'd run to him, not knowing what she needed, but only knowing that she hurt and that he might make it all better.

No, that wasn't true. She knew he couldn't fix things. He couldn't snap his fingers and make Meredith the woman she'd been. Say a few magic words and bring the sunshine back to what had once been this place of joy. Heal her scar, destroy the nightmares, show her a new path away from the sadness and into the sun.

Propped on one elbow, River lightly brushed Sophie's tangled hair away from her cheek, exposing the scar that meant nothing to him, so very much to her. Would the day ever come when she realized that the scar was so much less important than the way she saw herself? He hated the way she hid the healing wound with her hair, deliberately ducked or turned her head when anyone looked at her.

He couldn't even hold her, tell her he loved her, because she wouldn't believe him. How could she? Had he gone after her when she left the ranch? Followed her to the city? Said so much as a single word when she'd shown up at the ranch with Chet Wallace's ring on her finger?

No. He hadn't. He'd done nothing. Time and time again, he'd let her go. Because he had nothing to offer her but his love, his dreams. Because his background was so clouded, his pride so stiff, his pockets so empty.

He'd had to fight through his own personal demons, his own private nightmares. The always-present feeling of being unwanted, unloved, rejected by those he loved. He'd held on to the anger that had sustained him.

And, most of all, he had the knowledge that he was a half-breed foster child who owed Joe and Meredith Colton everything he had and would ever have—including owing them what was best for their daughter.

Sophie had pestered him with her teenage crush, had maddened him as she grew into the most beautiful woman he'd ever hoped to see—both in face and form as well as in mind and spirit.

He'd done that for her, in his way. He'd pushed her away, forced her to leave, go to school, grow up.

But he'd never thought she would come home with another man's ring on her finger.

That was when he'd finally gone to Joe, his bankbook in hand, and asked to purchase fifty acres of the sprawling ranch for his own house and stables, to begin his own stud, board and horse training operation. Because he needed something of his own in order to be able to give it all to Sophie. He needed to be his own man, a man who could look Joe Colton in the eye while he asked for Sophie's hand in marriage. A man who could promise that he'd always care for her, protect her, keep her safe—and mean it.

River smiled a crooked, lopsided smile as he traced Sophie's slim bare shoulder with his fingertips, wondering what she'd think if he took her out to his land, if she could see the house he was building, the stables that were already complete, waiting for the horses he'd purchase.

She'd be pleased for him, he was certain of that much. But would she believe that he had done it not just for himself, but for her? Would she believe that he spent his nights dreaming of Sophie waiting in their own house as he walked up from the stables? Would she believe that he could close his eyes and see the two of them riding along together on their horses, or sitting in the swing he would build for their front porch, or smiling down together at the face of the child they would make?

His smile widened ruefully as he shook his head and chuckled low in his throat. Sure. She'd believe all of that. Right after she horsewhipped him. Because timing was all, as some wise man said, and his timing was lousy. Really, really lousy.

Sophie stirred next to him, and he watched as her eyes opened, then widened in horror, as her entire body went stiff with shock. "Oh, God," she moaned, turning her face into the pillows. "Oh, Sophie, you've really done it this time. Wasn't once enough? How do you explain this one to yourself?"

Obviously, she thought she was alone. "Good morning, Soph," River said, and she moaned again, buried her face even deeper into the pillow. "Sleep well?"

"Go to hell," she mumbled, pulling the pillow out from under her and then jamming it over her head. She kicked back at his legs, one bare foot connecting with his right shin. "Go away. Just go away."

River made a face that Sophie once would have laughed at, called comical. "I knew it," he said, rolling out of the bed, reaching for his jeans. "The morning-after-the-night-before remorse. Sophie, if you weren't so predictable, I think I'd be insulted."

"I don't care if you *are* insulted," she said, her voice still faintly muffled, but her tone easily interpreted. "Just let me hear the door close, with you standing on the other side of it."

"Okay. Want some coffee? Bacon and eggs? Crow?"

"No!"

"In that case, I think I'll go down to the stables and take a ride."

"Do that," Sophie told him flatly, and he walked over to the door, shut it, then watched as she slid out of the bed, dragging the sheet with her as she wrapped it, toga-style, around her slim body.

She stopped halfway to the bathroom. Her spine went straight and stiff and she slowly turned around and glared at him. "You rat!"

"And you're beautiful," he answered. "All rosy and warm, with your hair tangled around your face. I don't suppose...?"

"Right. You don't," Sophie agreed, her smile reluctant, but there. And then the smile fled, as she raised a hand to hide her cheek. Without another word, she disappeared into the bathroom, the sound of the lock tumbling into place echoing like a rifle shot in River's brain.

"Couldn't find anyone else, huh?" River said, opening the door to the SUV so that Sophie could walk past him, her chin in the air, and climb up on the seat.

"Not for lack of trying," she answered under her breath, turning her face forward as he closed the door and walked around to the driver's side of the vehicle.

It was Monday afternoon, and Sophie had indeed spent the morning asking anyone and everyone if some one of them could please, *please* drive her to Prosperino for her physical therapy session.

She never knew everybody else could be so damn busy, so full of reasons why they couldn't take two hours off to help her out.

"I know I took you all last week, Sophie," Emily had told her, already heading for the front door, car keys in her hand. "But I really do have to go over to Hopechest and help Rebecca. I promised. Besides, I thought River was supposed to be driving you."

Amber had responded to a knock on her bedroom door, her strawberry-blond hair folded up in several dozen envelopes of plastic wrap. "Sorry," she'd said, shrugging. "Just putting in a few little highlights. I can't go to town like this, or everyone will know my natural sun-streaking sometimes gets a little help from a bottle. Besides, I thought River was supposed to be driving you."

By the time her father had begged off because he was waiting for an important international phone call—this man who hadn't paid much attention to business in a long time—and ended his refusal with "Besides, I thought River was supposed to be driving you," Sophie had begun to sense a trend.

And a plot.

Not that she was going to say so to him. She wasn't going to say *boo* to River James. Why, she wouldn't speak to him if her hair caught on fire and he was holding the only container of water within fifty miles.

She held it in, zipped it up and kept her silence…for fifteen long, excruciating minutes.

"You did it, didn't you? You told everybody to find something else to do so that you *had* to drive me," she accused, turning on the seat to glare at him. "Admit it. You did, didn't you?"

River turned his head toward her and waggled his eyebrows. "I cannot tell a lie. I chopped down the cherry tree. I did it with my little hatchet."

Sophie growled low in her throat. "That's not funny," she told him, tightly folding her arms across her chest. "And you're no George Washington."

"That's good, because I think he's pretty old," River responded, pulling his cowboy hat slightly lower over his forehead. "I know. I'll be John Paul

Jones. What was it he said? 'I have not yet begun to fight.' Yeah. That's good. And it fits. I'll be him.''

''Well, you're half right. You'll be history, that's what you'll be, if you don't stop interfering in my life,'' Sophie declared hotly. ''I'd rather walk to therapy than have you drive me.''

''If you could walk to therapy, Soph, you wouldn't *need* therapy,'' River pointed out maddeningly. He slowed the SUV, heading toward the shoulder of the road. ''However, if you want to try…''

''Don't you dare stop this car!'' Sophie exploded, then pressed her head back against the seat. ''Oh, I give up. I give up, Riv. I know better than to fight with you. You don't play fair, and never have.''

''I play to win, Soph,'' he told her, pulling back onto the blacktop, stepping on the gas. ''You, however, don't play at all anymore.''

''Life isn't a game.''

''No, sweetheart,'' River said as he pulled into the parking lot, ''it most definitely is not. We both know that, don't we? Life is, however, to be lived.''

''Meaning?'' she asked, wishing she didn't feel compelled to ask.

''Meaning you're not living right now, Soph. You're hiding. Hiding from people because of that scar, because that mugger made you distrust everyone who comes within ten feet of you—strangers and family alike. Meaning you're going to keep Meredith's secret, not because she asked, but because you're afraid of what might happen if Joe and the rest of you were at last forced to face the truth, that Meredith is slowly losing her mind. Meaning, Soph, that you and I have something real between us, something you can't ignore, much as you want to…and sooner or later you're going to have to face up to that as well. Now go get your therapy. I'll be back in an hour.''

Sophie blinked back tears as she blindly reached for the door handle. ''And who told you that you were qualified to hang out your shingle, *Dr.* James? Some psychologist you are. You can't even run your own life.''

She opened the door, but River's hand on her arm stopped her from exiting the vehicle. ''Oh, no, you don't, Soph. You don't make a crack like that and then run off. What's wrong with my life?''

Sophie turned, glared at him and smiled evilly. ''You're kidding, right?''

''Sophie…''

''Oh, all right. Okay. Tell me this, Mr. Lone Wolf. When was the last time you let anyone close to you? Other than your sister, Cheyenne? Huh? Talk about *trust.* You don't trust anyone, Riv. You're always waiting for someone to leave you, so much so that, when they don't leave, you push them away. Your mother died and left you, your grandmother took Rafe and Cheyenne—but not you. Your father beat you, so that the authorities took you away—and your father never came back, never tried to make amends. Hell, he was probably glad to see you gone, right? Isn't that how you figured it to be?''

''Sophie, don't do this.''

''Don't do this? Why not? You're so busy telling *me* what's wrong with *me.* Why not you, Riv? You came to the ranch, nasty and angry and prickly, and everybody tippy-toed around you, giving you room, giving you space. Poor River. Poor, poor River. Tread carefully with him, everyone. He's got issues. I damn near broke my neck trying to get close to you, and then all you did in the end was push me away.''

''You needed to go. You needed some experiences in life. College. You had dreams, Sophie.''

''And you didn't? You never dreamed of me, Riv? You never wanted *me*?''

''You know I did. I do.''

Sophie shook her head violently. ''Tell yourself anything you want, Riv. But don't lie to me. Everybody on the ranch was afraid of you. The loner, the hothead, the troubled kid, and now the hard, and hard-to-read man. You pushed us all away, kept us all at a distance. You did it then, quite obviously, and you still do it now, only you're more subtle. You're thirty-one years old, Riv. When are you going to figure out that people love you, that they aren't going to leave you? When are *you* going to stop being afraid of *me?* Not that you could ever love me, Riv. You don't know how to love anyone.''

River let go of her arm, which was the only reason Sophie realized he'd still been holding her there, in the vehicle. She looked at him for long moments, saw the pain in his face. Pain she had put there.

''Don't bother to pick me up. I'm a big girl now. I know how to call a cab.'' Sophie then took a quick, sharp, painful breath, and left him there.

Thirteen

"Thank you, Inez," Meredith called out over her shoulder, belatedly, she knew, but it always seemed to take her some time to remember things like "please" and "thank you" when the woman was only doing what Joe Colton paid her to do.

After all, Inez Ramirez and her family had a roof over their heads, food in their bellies and a job security most of the world would give their eyeteeth to have. Which, of course, wasn't enough for them, was it? Now one of Inez's little senoritas, Maya, had gotten her hooks into Drake and, as it followed, would soon be dug deep into the Colton money.

"Over my dead body," Meredith assured herself, reaching for the stack of mail Inez had brought to her in her sitting room. "Isn't it enough we've already got the half-breed sniffing after Sophie? That's what happens when you bring home strays, you stupid, stupid man. You have two sons that are worthy of the Colton fortune, and only two, not that you see that, of course. Joe Colton, you're the stupidest man alive.''

Meredith took a deep breath, reminding herself that it did her no good to become upset. After all, it would all change soon enough. Everything would change soon, and most definitely for the better.

She sorted through the mail, first picking out all the last few RSVP envelopes, smiling as she read the return addresses, sliced open the envelopes and saw all the positive responses, not that she had expected anyone to turn her down.

Look who was in today's batch of responses: Senator Howard, Representative Blakely and Mrs. Reginald Walker, III, a high-nosed widow who was a leading hostess in San Francisco. She frowned as she saw the overseas stamp on the envelope from Joe's Aunt Sybil, then put it with the others. Oh, well, at least Paris would be represented. She supposed that was a fair enough trade-off for having to put up with Sybil and her nosy, interfering ways.

Less than three weeks, and it would be party time. Oh, my oh my, she thought, would it ever!

Meredith picked up the remainder of the mail addressed to her and frowned as she realized she'd overlooked the most important letter, the one that had arrived without a return address and was marked Personal and Confidential.

Suppressing the urge to rip the envelope in her

haste, she carefully slit the top with the silver letter opener and withdrew the contents.

"My dear Mrs. Colton," the letter began, and she sniffed derisively at the intimacy of the salutation. As if the man was her dear anything!

It is with regret that I inform you that the lead I followed up on last month has led to yet another dead end. I have found no trace of the subject, Patricia Portman, either here or in Nevada, as we had hoped. "Patty Portmann," is Caucasian, brown-eyed, brown-haired, medium height and build, fifty-two years of age, as we knew fit the criteria. However, she has lived in Las Vegas all of her life; maiden name Patty Schlenker. Interviews with neighbors and relatives confirmed all of this to my satisfaction.

This is our fifth dead end after high hopes, Mrs. Colton, and I hesitate to suggest that you continue the search, as I do not wish to incur any more expenses on your behalf when I can offer so little hope that I will be able to locate your missing sister.

"Here comes the *however,*" Meredith muttered under her breath, and sure enough, there it was.

However, if you were to give me permission, I would like to follow the one remaining lead we have, that being the Mississippi address you forwarded to me last month. Only you know if this is a viable lead, so I leave it up to you to decide whether or not it should be followed.

The usual rates would apply. Seventy dollars an hour, plus all airfare and living expenses.

Meredith mentally wrote another five-figure check, wondering how many more she could write before Joe decided to take an interest in her personal account. He'd been so oblivious, for so long. But now he seemed to be taking an interest again, coming out of his stupor, his depression.

Dangerous. Very dangerous. Dangerous enough to give the detective the address she'd hoped never to have to use, just in case the man had more brains than she so far gave him credit for possessing. Locating her sister was one thing, exposing herself was another—and definitely not acceptable. She would much rather the detective located the Mississippi address on his own, so that it couldn't be connected with her in any way.

All of this was just another reason, of so many reasons, to give Joe Colton a fine and very final bon voyage on his sixtieth birthday. She was tired of hiding, tired of worrying. Tired of fearing discovery.

She read on:

As to that other matter, again I am sorry to say that I have had little success. There was a female infant adopted that same week, but she was not the only infant placed for private adoption in that week or the one following. In total, three female infants, ranging in age from newborn to two months—if we can believe what we hear—were adopted in the hundred-mile area I checked.

Broadening the search to a two hundred-mile radius, there are a total of fifteen Caucasian female infants who were placed for adoption and/or foster care in the two months following the date you gave me. All female Caucasian infant deaths reported in that time have been checked out and eliminated, which is the only good news I have for you, I'm afraid.

Time is our enemy, as tracking records that date back more than thirty years is complicated at best, and the records are often still under seal. New laws have opened some records, but adoptive parents retain many rights, as do adoptive children, so that records can still be held secret. I already know that you'll wish for me to continue my search in this matter, and will report to you monthly, as always, sooner if there should be any new information. Please find my enclosed bill for services rendered to date.

Meredith looked at the bill, then crumpled it in her hand and flung it across the room. "Idiot! He's been at this for a year. All of them, all the idiots I've hired and fired. They couldn't find their own behinds with their own two hands!"

She stood up slowly, feeling stiff and defeated. She needed to find Patsy. She *had* to find Jewel.

She had to get rid of Joe Colton and his sniveling bunch of strays, so that she'd be free to do both.

Meredith picked up the private detective's bill and

smoothed it between her hands. She'd pay it. She'd pay and she'd pay and she'd pay. She'd do anything, *anything,* to find her Jewel. Anything to find and destroy Patsy.

Anything to be safe.

After all, *she* was Meredith Colton. Only her, no one else. Everybody knew that.

A slow smile lit Meredith's face as she entered the bathroom, drew out her small brown bottle of pills. Have to keep taking the pills, at least for now. Keep calm. Stay safe. Afterward she'd flush them all down the toilet, flush that quack doctor down with them.

She wasn't insane. She was the most sane person she knew. It was the world that had gone crazy. The whole system was insane. Seeking supposedly legal vengeance for the death of a lying, useless piece of male trash. Punishing a mother for trying to find where that cold monster had put her very own newborn child. Locking up that mother for years and years, telling her she was sick and needed help.

Help? Yes, she needed help. But not the kind those quack doctors meant.

Meredith went back into the sitting room and withdrew a small key from her pocket, unlocking her desk drawer. She lifted out the small, folded piece of paper that held a name and the phone number for a fleabag hotel. A name she had gone to the slums of Los Angeles to learn. A name she had paid dearly to obtain. A man who could point her toward yet another man, a man who would do anything she asked, if the color of her money was right.

Did she dare? Could she do it? Could she afford

not to do it? Was the time right to bring in help that wasn't shackled by ethics or whatever it was that the private investigators she'd hired had all grumbled about?

She had one name, which would lead her to another name, to a man who could solve the rest of her problems for her. All she had to do was take that second step, the one that would put her face to face with a potential murderer.

After the party. She'd find him after the party, bring him into the picture when the household was already in shock, dealing with their grief. Why drag it out? Why make them deal with the grief twice? She could be nice, considerate. She'd get all the wailing and sobbing over with at the same time. Joe, dead. Emily, dead.

Whiny, talk-too-much, question-too-much, "I saw two mommies" Emily.

Oh, yes. One by one, they'd be gone, gone, gone.

"Ten little, nine little, eight worthless Coltons...seven little, six little, five no-good Coltons..." Meredith laughed, then quickly clapped both her hands over her mouth to keep that laugh from escalating into hysteria. She had to be careful. So careful.

Soon there would be only two. Her boys. Her very own boys.

And—if that idiot detective would just get on the stick—her Jewel...

"You look like you've been rode hard and put away wet," Joe Colton said, opening the door to River's small apartment and stepping inside.

River, who had been sitting on the couch, unmindful of the trail dust that clung to him after his hell-bent-for-leather gallop over the fields, merely grunted, lifted the long-neck beer to his lips and drank deeply.

Joe picked up the two empty brown beer bottles sitting on the coffee table. "That's just about your limit, don't you think, son?"

River grumbled low in his throat. "White man's firewater bad for the Red Man, *Kemo Sabé*," he muttered, inwardly wincing at his own juvenile sarcasm. He slowly lifted his head and looked at his foster father. "I'm sorry, Joe. Really. That was uncalled for."

"It certainly was. It was an insult to your mother's people, to yourself, and probably to me." He took the chair that sat at a right angle to the couch. "Want to talk about it?"

"Not particularly, no," River said with a faint smile. "Is she home yet? Or did she run all the way back to the city, putting as much space between the two of us as she can?"

"Oh, she's back. I saw the taxi drive up myself, about two hours ago. I asked her why you hadn't brought her home and she said she wouldn't cross the street with you. Nice. I take it you two had a small argument?"

"World War Two was a small argument, Joe," River told him facetiously. "We had us one great big, whacking, thermonuclear war. Didn't you see the mushrooms clouds? They had to be kind of hard to miss."

"You love her very much, don't you?"

River rubbed at his chin. "Yeah. Yeah, I do. For all the good it's doing me."

Joe sighed, folded his large hands in his lap. "I remember when I met Meredith." He shook his head. "God, so many years ago, and yet sometimes it feels like yesterday. Did I ever tell you the story?"

He had, but River decided that Joe needed to tell it again, that he needed to remember the good days, the good times. "No," River said. "But I'd love to hear it. Let me get us some coffee, all right?"

River came back into the room a few minutes later, to see Joe sitting low in the chair, his chin on his chest.

"Here you go. Black, with two sugars, since Inez isn't around to make you use that funny stuff."

Joe looked up, his eyes blank for a moment, and then smiled, accepted the cup. "She's going to have me out in the fields grazing pretty soon. I'm going to be sixty, not ninety, you know. You'd think she'd let me wallow in my fats and sugars for at least another few years."

"Inez cares about you, Joe. That physical you had six months ago shook us all up. Cholesterol too high, overweight, your loss of energy…"

"I didn't ask for a list," Joe bit out, then sighed. "You forgot depressed. As if there'd be anyone who wouldn't be depressed, damn it. Meredith—"

"Yes," River interrupted quickly. "You were going to tell me how the two of you met."

Joe sniffed, shook his head. "You're good at this, River. I'm surprised you can't talk to Sophie for more than two minutes without thermonuclear war."

"My talents only reach so far," River admitted, smiling wryly. "But maybe I can learn from you. Tell me, how did you woo and win the fair Meredith? I mean, there you were, this great big lump—" River's smile broadened "—and there she was, this sweet, gentle lady."

Joe sipped at his coffee, then set the cup down on the table. "She was, you know. A sweet, gentle lady. Most definitely a lady."

He looked across at River, who had retaken his own seat on the couch. "She had car trouble. Graham and I were driving along, heading for some business function. Just outside Sacramento we saw this car pulled over to the side of the road. Meredith was standing there, the hood open on her old, beat-up Chevy, as I remember, looking about as helpless as a babe lost in the woods. But beautiful. God, she was beautiful. They wore miniskirts back in those days. Hers was blue mostly, with some kind of flowers on it, not that I noticed. I was way too busy looking at her legs. Long, bare, tanned legs. I damn near tripped over myself trying to get to her first, but Graham beat me to it."

"Your brother's a little smaller, could probably move faster," River said as Joe paused, obviously lost in a mental picture of how Meredith had looked when he'd seen her for the first time. Her appearance had probably been one hell of a hit to Joe's solar plexus, rather like the one River knew he had felt the first time he'd seen Sophie. Hard to believe, he supposed, but even then he'd known. He'd always known. With a woman like Meredith, like her daughter, one look was all it would take to have a man love her forever.

"My little brother was a little faster in a lot of ways, River," Joe said, bringing River back from his own musings. "Before I knew what happened, I had my head stuck under the hood, fixing the problem, and he was asking for—and getting—her phone number. They made a date for that same night."

"Ouch," River said, knowing the story, but still enjoying it. "Did you have to beat him up?"

"No, but not because the thought hadn't crossed my mind. I mean, I really thought Meredith looked surprised that Graham asked for her number. She was looking at me, really looking at me, and she seemed disappointed that I hadn't asked, that Graham had. But then Graham screwed up, thank God."

Joe took another drink of coffee and wet his dry lips. "You see, Graham only asked for Meredith's number because that was a sort of natural reflex for him. See a beautiful woman, ask her out. And never mind that he already had a date for that night, with some secretary he'd met on his last trip to Sacramento. Real hot stuff, to hear Graham tell it. Anyway, he went off to meet the secretary, promising to be back in time to meet Meredith in our hotel lobby at nine o'clock."

"Gives a whole new meaning to the term 'double-date,' doesn't it?" River asked, knowing it was an old joke.

"Graham was pretty irresponsible in those days," Joe admitted. "And, you know, I didn't really know him all that well at the time. When our parents died, he was sent to live with our grandparents, and I was shipped out here, to live with the McGraths, my father's old army buddy. We'd only gotten back in touch with each other a little while earlier, when I asked him to join me in the business."

River nodded, keeping his opinions to himself. He knew that Joe had been rejected by his mother's parents, who believed his father's drunkenness had caused their daughter's as well as his own death in an automobile accident.

He knew that Joe, who resembled his father physically, had been turned away, while Graham, whose finely boned body and lighter coloring was much like his mother's, had been raised in the lap of luxury— until the money ran out and Graham suddenly remembered he had a brother, a brother who was doing quite well, thank you. River adored Joe, because Joe knew what it was like to be rejected. Joe had told him his story while River still lived at Hopechest Ranch, gaining his trust and forming a bond that would never break.

At the same time, River disliked Graham Colton on general principles, because the man was lazy and sly. Conniving. Opportunistic. Jealous. Not that Joe saw any of it or, if he did, wanted to believe it.

Joe drained his cup of coffee, then continued with his story. "Nine o'clock came and went, and Graham never showed up. Meredith called up to our rooms, to see where he was, and I finally, *finally,* got up the nerve to go after her myself. I met her downstairs after leaving a note for Graham, and the two of us had dinner at the hotel."

He closed his eyes, smiled. "My God, River, we talked for hours. About how she was going to the university to become a teacher, about how much she loved children. I think I heard every third word, though, to tell you the truth. I just kept getting lost in those big brown eyes of hers, that bright, beautiful smile."

"Yeah. I know the feeling," River interjected, pulling a face. "It's those eyes. You can actually see her dreams in those big, brown eyes."

"By the time Graham showed up, all full of apologies, Meredith and I had already made plans to see each other the next day. God, I was a wreck. A nervous wreck. There I was, twenty-seven years old, and I had absolutely no idea how to go about wooing a woman. But it didn't matter. Meredith had this way of getting me to talk. About myself, my family, my hopes, my dreams. I mean, by the time Graham showed up that first night, we knew so much about each other, liked so much about each other, that it was as if he wasn't even there. He was sort of angry for a while, but he got over it, was best man at our wedding a year later."

River sat forward, his elbows on his knees. "Ever wonder how it would have worked out if Graham had come back to the hotel on time? Do you think he ever wonders about that?"

Joe shook his head. "I don't think so. Oh, he used to tease me sometimes, say that not only did we break his heart, but that I'd never really been all that successful until Meredith came into my life—and that if he had married her, maybe he'd be the one who owned Colton Enterprises. But that was just teasing. He never really meant it.''

"No, I suppose not," River said, then changed the subject. "But you know, Joe, you never really told me how you got Meredith to love you, believe you loved her.''

"I didn't?'' Joe frowned, rubbed at the back of his neck. "I guess I never really thought about it. We just...clicked. Oh, not that we didn't have our fights, because we did. But we knew the love was there. We always knew the love was there, in the good times, in the bad times. I'll never forget that, River. I *can't* forget that. And I can't give up.''

After Joe left, River cleaned up the beer bottles and coffee cups and headed for the shower, intent on ridding himself of his dirt and dust, clearing his head by sticking it under a stinging spray of hot water.

He had stripped down to his briefs when he noticed. The bag, the white plastic bag from the pharmacy that Sophie had refused to take with her the day he'd bought a half dozen different pregnancy test kits, was gone.

He'd put it on the shelf above the commode, he was sure he had.

He looked in the cabinet under the sink, then in the small linen closet in the bathroom. Nothing.

He searched his entire apartment, all the closets, the kitchen cabinets, the trash can outside, at the bottom of the stairs.

Nothing.

The bag was gone. Sophie had been in the bathroom yesterday morning after throwing him out of his own apartment. Had she seen the bag? Could she have taken the bag?

Why had she taken the bag?

River squeezed his eyes shut, roughly scrubbed at the back of his neck with one hand. Was this a good thing? Or a bad thing?

If she wasn't pregnant, would that make it easier for him to finally convince her that he loved her?

If she was pregnant, how in hell could he ever get her to believe that he loved her and wanted to marry her?

"Safe sex," he said, stripping out of his briefs and turning on the shower. "Man, they aren't kidding when they say it's the only smart way."

Fourteen

Sophie stomped toward the stables, still wondering if she should make a list of all the reasons River James should be tarred, feathered and run out of town on a rail.

She could start with the fact that he'd left her alone at physical therapy six days ago. Sure, she'd told him to, but did he have to listen to her?

Number two on the list would have to be the way he'd been ignoring her ever since she'd opened her big mouth and said so many nasty, unforgivable things to him. Okay, so some of them might have been true, at least at some point in his life, but they both knew she was only striking out at him, deliberately trying to hurt him.

Three, definitely, was that he wouldn't let her apologize, damn it. He'd gone away Tuesday morning, to some horse show somewhere, and hadn't come back until Thursday night. She'd dressed for dinner with such care, such anticipation, and he hadn't shown up, hadn't come up to the house a single time since he'd returned from the show.

That was just plain despicable of him! It wasn't as if she wanted to go down to the stables to confront him. He was making her do it. He had to know that she couldn't stand the way things had been left between them and needed to talk to him, that she would finally break down and go after him.

What was four? There had to be a four. There had to be a ten, and a twelve, and a forty-seven. She had *so* many reasons to be angry with him.

And a million reasons to be angry with herself, ashamed of herself—although she wouldn't think about that now, or she'd lose her courage, turn around and go hide in her room with the covers over her head.

"Drake?" she asked, seeing her brother walking toward her along the road leading from the stables. "Have you been to the stables? Is River down there?"

"River?" Drake shook his head. "No, Soph, he's not. I think he's at the house."

Sophie shook her head. "No, he's not. I just came from there."

"You did? What do you think of it? It's small, but he planned it sort of like our place—with a two-story central area, and room to put wings on each side later on."

Sophie made a face and looked at her brother quizzically. "What are you talking about?"

"The house. River's house," Drake said, then smiled slowly as he realized she didn't have the faintest idea what he was talking about. He said so: "You don't have the faintest idea what I'm talking about, do you?"

She shook her head, unable to find her voice.

"I wonder why he didn't— Yeah, well, none of my business, right? Very military, with River doling out information on a need-to-know basis," Drake said, then proceeded to tell her all about River's purchase of land, the house he was building, the stable that was already completed, the business he planned to start in the next month or so. "And he didn't tell you?"

"No," Sophie said shortly, blinking back tears. "I—I suppose it was going to be a...surprise. Oh, well, not that it matters. Thanks for the information, Drake. I never did much like surprises."

She brushed past him, still heading for the stables.

"Where are you going, Soph? I already told you, Riv isn't there," her brother called after her.

"Riding. I'm going riding," she said, having made up her mind at exactly that moment. "The therapist said I could if I wanted to, so I'm going to take a ride."

"You know where you're going?" Drake asked.

"Oh, yeah," she muttered as she nodded and waved at Drake, all the while still heading for the stables. "I sure do."

Reason number four: She didn't have to have reasons. All she had to do was *think* about River James, and her blood began to boil!

Louise sat in her favorite deck chair, but didn't look comfortable. Her feet were both firmly on the brick patio, her knees close together. Her hands gripped the arms of the chair, her knuckles white with strain. Her mouth was pinched, her breathing shallow.

"Louise, relax," Dr. Wilkes said, taking up her own seat in a folding chair she'd placed in front of her patient. "I'm not going to take you too deep, I promise."

"I know," Louise said, sighing, looking at the fountain that sat silent on the patio. "But—but what if the bad me comes out? What if she stays out?"

Martha Wilkes nodded, expecting the question, then chose her words carefully. "Louise, we aren't yet sure yours is a multiple personality disorder. Remember? You fit some of the criteria, but not all of them. That's why I want to hypnotize you, take you back, search your memory. Because this could be amnesia, you know. Some sort of trauma-induced, injury-induced amnesia."

"Yes, you did say that. But amnesia? Isn't that just in movies and books?"

"I'll agree that it is just as rare as multiple personalities, surely, but it is just as possible. We've done all the usual—years of talk, personality testing, of building trust between us, and we've made progress. But not much, especially as you spent most of those years fighting me even while asking for my help. We're at a dead end, and this is probably the last way still open to us. We've agreed on that. Now, the only thing left is—do you trust me, Louise?''

Louise wet her dry lips with the tip of her tongue and tried to smile. "You know I trust you, Martha. All right, let's try it. Turn it on. Since I haven't been brave enough to do it myself in this past week, we might as well try to get some use out of the thing."

Martha reached down and flicked the switch that turned on the fountain, deliberately keeping her expression blank as Louise flinched at the sight and sound of the cascading water. "All right, Louise, look at the water. How soothing it is. It's so pretty. Isn't it pretty, Louise?"

"Pretty," Louise agreed, relaxing her death grip on the chair arms, then folding her hands together in her lap.

"Yes. So pretty. So relaxing. You're relaxing, aren't you, Louise? All the cares, all the worries fading. Fading. Leaving you. And the sound. Oh, what a lovely sound. Gentle, like rain on a spring morning, as you lie in bed, smiling, turning over to go back to sleep. Are you sleepy, Louise? Your eyelids are heavy. Why don't you close your eyes, Louise? That's it. Close your eyes, listen to the water. Listen to the water and my voice. There's nothing else, Louise, nothing but the water and my voice."

Louise's eyes fluttered, then closed.

Dr. Wilkes closed her own eyes for a moment, collecting her own thoughts, calming her own jangled nerves. She and Louise had been working at relaxation the entire week, so that it was now almost amazingly easy to lead her patient where she wanted her to go. "All right, Louise," she said after a moment. "We're going to go back now. Back to that other garden, to that other fountain. Do you see them? Do you see the garden? Do you see the fountain?"

Nodding, Louise said quietly, "Yes. Yes, I do see them. I see them both."

"Are you there? Are you in the garden, Louise? Do you see yourself there?"

"Yes."

"Wonderful. What are you doing, Louise? What are you doing in the garden?"

"Singing," Louise said, a slight smile curving her mouth. "I'm singing. We're both singing." Her smile widened, even as she kept her eyes closed. "'Yankee Doodle went to town, riding on a pony...'"

"Oh, that's nice, Louise. I always liked that song. A children's song. Is that who's with you? A child?"

Louise's brow furrowed and she shut her eyelids tighter. "A little girl. Oh, she looks like me," she said, her voice breaking, her expression one of incredible, aching sadness. "She looks just like me."

"But she's not you, is she, Louise? She's a little girl. Who is she, Louise? Can you ask her to tell you her name?"

Cocking her head to one side, Louise seemed to be listening to something. "I—I can't hear her. She's still singing. 'Put a feather in his hat, and called it Macaroni.' Isn't that silly? Who'd call a feather Macaroni? Yes, it is funny. We're both laughing..."

"Is she done now? Louise, is she done singing now?" Dr. Wilkes asked after a few moments, moments in which she watched the beatific smile on her patient's face, her own heart breaking for the woman.

"What's your name, little girl?" Louise asked. "Why do you look like me? Why are we singing?"

Louise was taking charge of the session, asking her own questions. Dr. Wilkes held her breath, knowing that disturbing Louise now could ruin everything. So she waited, watched as Louise listened yet again and nodded.

"That's a pretty name. Aren't you lucky to have such a pretty name. That was my grandmother's name."

Dr. Wilkes's eyebrows shot up in surprise. Not only the child's name, but the grandmother's? This was progress. She decided it was safe to push Louise just a little harder. "Louise, would you please ask the little girl who she is? Why is she in the garden with you? Why were you two singing together?"

She realized her mistake as soon as the words were out of her mouth, just as Louise's posture became stiff, guarded. Too far, too fast! Why had she pushed? "Louise? Don't ask her, not yet. Just be in the garden, Louise. Sing with the little girl. Enjoy the moment, go back into the moment."

Louise's eyes opened wide, and Dr. Wilkes could see the fear in their depths. "What happened? Where did the little girl go? I don't want you here. You don't belong here. *I* belong here, not you. Not you!"

"Louise!" Dr. Wilkes said, her voice strong as she tried to regain control of her patient. "It's time to come back, time to leave the garden."

"Mama said not to talk about you," Louise continued, lost inside her own mind. "She said you were sick, that we had to obey you, not see you. Forget you. I didn't want to, but it was for the best, wasn't it? It's what *you* wanted. I wanted to tell him, but the time was never right. And now it's too late. You're dead. I have the letter from that place they sent you to. It says so in the letter. They told me you were dead. Don't look like me. I *hate* that you look like me! Talk to me, Patsy. *Patsy, what are you doing in my garden!*"

"Louise! Louise!" Dr. Wilkes repeated, turning off the fountain. "That's enough. Listen to me, only to me. You're coming back now…"

Dr. Wilkes went through all the procedures she'd learned, telling Louise to relax, that she would wake now, refreshed, not fearful. Then she brought her out of the trance, greatly relieved when Louise blinked a few times, then opened her eyes once more and asked, "What happened? Did I say anything?"

"No, not much," Dr. Wilkes said, knowing this wasn't the time for a rehashing of all that had just transpired. "We just visited the garden, that's all. We're going to go slowly, Louise. Take this one step at a time."

Louise nodded, then stood up, went to the nearby picnic table to pour them each a glass of lemonade.

"What's your grandmother's name, Louise?" Dr. Wilkes asked, employing the same casual tone she would use to inquire about Louise's feelings concerning whether or not they'd have rain by that evening.

Louise continued to pour lemonade into the glasses. "My grandmother's name? It's Sophie. Why?"

"No reason," Dr. Wilkes said, then waited until Louise realized what she'd said. It didn't take long.

One of the glasses tipped over, lemonade running across the tabletop, dripping onto the bricks below. Louise ignored the spill as she turned to look at the doctor. "Martha? How did I know that? I never knew that before. I know I didn't. I don't remember *anything* about my family."

Dr. Wilkes shrugged. "Sometimes, after a session, a memory or two will pop up unexpectedly. I just thought I'd give it a shot. It's nothing to concern you. Do you want help cleaning up that mess?"

Louise frowned, turned to look at the spilled lemonade. "Oh, I didn't even realize! I'll go inside and get some paper towels."

Dr. Wilkes nodded, but remained where she was, trying to sort through everything that had happened.

Sophie. The little girl's name was Sophie. What was her last name?

And Louise had said "him" again. A man, definitely a man, who played some very large role in Louise's life, at some point, at some time. But who was he?

Possibly more important—how had Patsy shown up in the garden? A fully grown Patsy, if Martha had interpreted Louise's statements correctly. Patsy, which was Louise's real name. Patsy, a grown woman, a woman who looked just like Louise, *was* Louise, but who didn't belong in Louise's garden.

Dead? Louise had said Patsy was dead. She'd even hinted that she'd gotten a letter from somewhere— from St. James's?—that *told* her Patsy was dead.

Dead? Cured? Which was it? A notification of death...or a clean bill of health?

Dr. Wilkes rested her chin in her hand. This was going to take some thought. Had Louise seen her other personality in that garden? Or had she seen herself—her *other* self, her *bad* self, the one she'd tried so hard to forget? Was it amnesia? That diagnosis seemed more feasible than one of multiple personality, but Dr. Wilkes couldn't be sure. Not yet.

Whatever it was, whatever Louise had seen, Martha Wilkes knew they were getting closer. Finally, after years of therapy, they were getting closer. She knew one other thing, a promise she'd made to herself and to Louise—she wouldn't stop now, not until they had *all* the answers.

River walked from room to room, amazed at the progress the builders had made in the two weeks since he'd been to see the house.

He hadn't wanted to come out here, not while his future was so up in the air, not while Sophie was running hot and cold, so that he didn't know if telling her about the house was the best or the worst thing he could do.

Timing. Timing was everything. And if he'd just gone to Joe last year, asked for the loan then, gone after Sophie then, maybe by this time he and Sophie would have been married, perhaps even starting a family.

Instead, she'd been mugged, nearly killed. She'd just broken her engagement with Chet Wallace, she might be pregnant with River's child, and she hated his guts.

He climbed the stairs two at a time, heading for the master suite. Well, not exactly a master suite, but definitely the largest of the three bedrooms, and the only one to have its own bath. The plumbing was in, complete, a clean, basic white. The bathtub and adjoining shower had been put in weeks ago, but that was because they'd been too large to leave until after other work had been done. Now the double sinks were in, the palest green countertops were on, the white wooden cabinets and brass hardware installed, and the white ceramic tile surrounding the tub and shower, repeated on the floor, was in and grouted. The brass faucets were installed and working.

It looked good. Better than he'd hoped. He wasn't too sure about the special tiles above the tub, two dozen hand-painted tiles arranged to make up a huge vase of colorful wildflowers, but the builder had said "the women really love this stuff."

River had a quick mental picture of Sophie in the oval tub. Up to the top of her breasts in bubbles, her shoulders wet and glistening, laughing and talking to him as he stood in front of one of the sinks before he took his shower, shaving his evening beard. She'd want him to shave his evening beard before they went to bed, so he wouldn't scrape her tender skin when he kissed her, loved her.

River shook his head, banishing the thought, and retraced his steps, coming out of the bedroom, heading back downstairs. Next week the walls would be painted, the random-plank hardwood floors would be varnished. The kitchen, except for the stove, which was still on order, was already done.

Nothing to do soon but move in, move out of the apartment above the stables, take himself almost two long miles away from Sophie, who couldn't run to his small apartment anymore in the middle of the night—to yell at him, cry all over him, or warm his lonely bed, his lonely heart.

An ending and a beginning. That was how some would see it, he supposed. He hoped Sophie didn't see it that way.

"I like it."

River turned abruptly, dropping the key he'd been about to put in the front door dead bolt. "Sophie?" he said in surprise, seeing her as she stood in the shade on the wide front porch, leaning against one of the pillars that held up the ranch style roof. "How…?"

"A little birdie whispered it in my ear," she told him, pushing away from the post. "Maybe not a blue-bird-type bird. Maybe a duck. Maybe a *male* duck. You do know how they can quack. Quack your ear right off."

"I guess I don't need any more of my twenty questions to figure out who you mean. Drake. You know, for a guy with a Top Secret clearance, he's got one very big mouth."

Sophie's smile faded. "You're just lucky I got all my anger out on the way here. Why didn't you tell me? Were you ever going to tell me?"

River didn't answer her. Instead, he picked up the

key he'd dropped, then opened the front door. "Would you like a tour?"

"Sure, why not? I've already checked out the stables. I left my horse there. Not as grand as the stables on the ranch, but very nice. Very nice."

"Thank you," River said, then winced. They were talking to each other like two casual acquaintances. Polite, kind, complimentary. He wanted to gag.

"You came out here on horseback? Who said you could ride again?" he asked, trying to get the conversation onto a more personal level, a more real level.

Sophie walked past him into the house. "My therapist, which you'd know, if you were ever around. I got permission after Wednesday's session. As a matter of fact, two more weeks, and they might spring me, because we've got the treadmill at home, and because I've proven to them that I'm good about doing my home exercises. Inez baked my favorite banana cake Thursday night, to celebrate. Of course, you weren't up to the house for dinner *that* night, either."

"Got any salt you want to pour in my wounds, Soph?" River asked, following after her as she walked through the living room and dining room, into the large country-style kitchen. "I'm sorry I didn't know."

"Uh-huh," Sophie murmured, walking over to the sink, looking out the window above it. "Great view. My condo sink is in front of a blank wall. I hate that. I like the floor, too," she said, scuffing her toe against the surface. "Is that real brick?"

"*Almost* real brick," River said. "I don't know the term, but it looks like brick, is stronger than brick, and is sealed so it cleans easily. A good idea, considering how I'll be tracking dirt in here all the time. Lord knows the mess I make in my apartment."

"And the words 'take off your cowboy boots' never entered your head?" Sophie asked, touching a finger against the in-the-door water and ice dispenser built into the refrigerator. Finally, when she had run out of things to touch, she turned around, pressed herself against the edge of the counter. She looked at him, then looked away and wet her lips. "So, what's upstairs?"

"You," River said quietly, "if only in my mind. Only you, Sophie."

She closed her eyes, sighed. "Yes…yes, well, I guess upstairs will have to wait for another time. I promised Rebecca and Emily that I'd…that I'd go to the movies with them tonight. So," she ended, pasting a bright, artificial smile on her face, "gotta run."

She took two steps forward before River took hold of her arm at the elbow. "We're going to work this out, aren't we, Soph?"

She bent her head, avoided his eyes. "Maybe. But—but not until I know."

River sighed, shook his head. "Have you taken one of those tests yet?"

"No," Sophie said, looking up at him, rolling her eyes, "I haven't 'taken one of those tests yet.' Just because I'm a little—"

She broke off, shut her mouth with a snap, so that River finished her sentence for her. "Just because you're a little *late,* Sophie? Is that what you're saying?''

She gave a sharp tug, got her arm free of his grip. "It's nothing! I had *trauma,* you jerk. My life has been turned upside down, more than once, too, in these past few weeks. You. Mom. This whole mess here at the ranch. You can't expect a body under stress to behave normally, you know.''

River tried to keep his expression blank, but just couldn't do it. "You could be pregnant, Soph. Couldn't you?''

"No, I could not!''

"Yes, you could. Admit it, you could be pregnant. Why don't you use one of those tests?''

Sophie's cheeks flushed a deep pink. "How can you even ask such a stupid question? I mean, if I am, then how could I ever know...really feel sure that you— Oh, damn! Leave me alone, River James. Just leave me alone!''

"Marry me, Soph. I keep asking, and I'll always keep asking. Please, marry me. Don't take the test, don't find out. Just marry me, now, and we'll take it from there.''

She shook her head, backed away from him. "I can't. I really, really can't. Not like this.''

She turned then, walked away, and he let her go. He was always letting her go. But this time he wouldn't let her get very far.

Timing. Timing was everything. And, by damn, this time he would get the timing right.

Fifteen

Anyone would think there was going to be a wedding at the Hacienda del Alegria. An entire downstairs room had been set aside, furnished with long tables to display the presents that were arriving at the house every day.

Not that there were any toasters or bread machines or blenders in the bunch. No, these were more the silver tray, mantel clock, gold pen and pencil set type gifts, those suitable to present to Senator Joseph Colton on the occasion of his sixtieth birthday.

Sophie walked in front of the linen-draped tables, shaking her head as she looked at a solid silver monogrammed boot jack—something her father would gawk at, laugh at, and then stuff in the back of his closet.

The saddle that had arrived yesterday, a gift from

the employees of their Texas radio and television station, had pleased Joe very much. "Happy trails, Senator," the small white card propped in front of the saddle read, and Sophie grinned as she remembered her father looking at the card, then saying, "My God, anyone would think I'm retiring. All I'm doing is turning sixty, which is bad enough, right, Soph?"

Sophie had gladly taken on the job of unpacking and arranging the gifts, keeping a notebook in which she listed each gift and who had sent it, in preparation for all the thank-you notes that would have to be written after the party.

It was fun, setting up the presents, displaying them to their best advantage. And it was, along with her three days a week physical therapy sessions in Prosperino and her home exercises that she faithfully did twice each day, another good reason to keep busy, stay away from the stables.

River was giving her room. Yes, that would be the proper term: he was giving her room. Room, and time, and she loved him for it. She was also surprised by it, because River had never struck her as a man with an endless supply of patience.

And he was sending her gifts. Every day, another gift. A bunch of wildflowers wrapped in pretty blue ribbon. Oval-shaped scented soaps arranged in a small wicker basket. A book on the culture of the Native American Indian. Rock candy in a paper bag that she recognized as coming from the general store halfway between the ranch and Prosperino—a place they had gone to for years, just for the rock candy.

The presents showed up in her room, on her bed,

every single day. She'd tried to catch him at it, but he varied the times of day, so that she'd always seen the presents but had never seen him.

It was possible that he was waiting for her to come to him, but she somehow doubted that. He would come to her, in his own time, in his own way.

What would happen then, however, was still anyone's guess. Especially after the results of the pregnancy test she'd taken the week after going to see him at his new house. The test she'd taken that day, and the next day, and all the days after that, until she'd run out of tests.

Sophie walked over to the table holding today's deliveries that still had to be unpacked, set up for display. There were six boxes today, one of which, if lifted and given a slight shake, promised to be a problem. She opened that one first.

Sure enough, the crystal decanter inside looked as if someone had punched a hole in its bulbous bottom, freeing small slivers of crystal to rattle around inside the box. She lifted the heavy crystal stopper, admired it, then set the entire box down, pushing it underneath the hanging tablecloth, figuring she'd deal with it later.

The next four boxes were opened, to reveal yet another silver tray, a framed, personally autographed print of Joe Montana—her father's favorite sports figure—a lovely set of six wineglasses, all with different colored stems and bases, and lastly, an intricately designed gold pocket watch that seemed capable of telling time on Mars as well as displaying the phases of the moon.

Wonderful gifts. Thoughtful gifts. Sophie smiled, because her father was a well-loved, well-respected man. Perhaps this outward display of affection from his friends and colleagues could make up, even in a small way, for the unhappiness he found in his own home.

The last box was small, rather heavy for its size, and Sophie frowned as she recognized the bold hand printing on the label.

"Chet? Chet sent a gift?" She hesitated, then reluctantly opened the sealed cardboard box, unwrapped the present inside. A paperweight. She lifted the heavy clear crystal globe out of the packing and smiled at the sixty-year-old twenty dollar gold piece embedded in the glass. Thoughtful, yes, but pretty much all show—and so very, very Chet. She looked into the box and found the small printed card: Happy sixtieth, Senator. I'm not able to attend your party, but am sure it will be the event of the year!

He'd signed the card with his name, and beneath that were the words *Wallace Enterprises, Ltd.*

"The ink on the check I wrote him could hardly be dry yet," Sophie told herself, carrying paperweight and card over to one of the display tables, "and he's already writing off gifts as a business expense." She made a face, silently scolded herself for her thoughts. Still, she knew, smiling, she was probably right. Chet would always land on his feet; the man wouldn't have it any other way.

Her chore done for the day, Sophie picked up the boxes, stuffing wrappings into a plastic bag, and then stacked the boxes inside each other. All she had to do now was carry the entire mess out to the recycling bins that were already overflowing, and then she could start her daily at-home exercises.

Deciding that the quickest way to the recycling bins was to cross the courtyard, Sophie exited the room via a set of French doors and put the boxes on the ground. She was just about to close the doors behind her when she heard voices. Somebody was coming into the room.

Because the French doors were on the sunniest side of the house, Meredith had ordered mini-blinds installed over the glass panes. The blinds were closed, so Sophie couldn't see into the room unless she opened the door all the way, and nobody could see her.

Not that it mattered. Not that she was going to eavesdrop or anything like that. But if it was her mother who was coming into the room…well, terrible as it might appear to anyone, Sophie was glad the woman wouldn't be able to see her. She just wasn't up to another round of Meredith's rapidly fluctuating moods. Not today, at least.

Just about to nudge the door closed quietly, so that nobody knew she was even there, Sophie's hand froze on the door latch as she heard her Uncle Graham say, ''If he finds out, Meredith, he'll kill us both, and you know it.''

''What do you want, Graham? Should I slit my wrist and write it in blood for you?'' Meredith asked peevishly. ''He isn't going to find out. Not from me, anyway. You're the one who can't seem to keep your mouth shut.''

"All right, all right, so maybe I'm just a little antsy, that's all. But he's been showing up at the office again, taking an interest. I like him better when he's down and out. He stays off my back when he's down and out."

"You can blame little run-home-to-papa Sophie for that one, Graham," Meredith said, her voice stronger, closer, so that Sophie backed away from the door, afraid her mother would see her. "She got herself all cut up, and Joe went ballistic. As if there was anything he could have done about it. Now he's taking an interest again. In his kids, in the business."

"Exactly! Something jolted him somehow. I wasn't sure what it was, but that does make sense. He nearly went crazy when Michael was killed, and blamed himself. He backed away from the business for a while, went into a funk for some of the happiest years of my life. Sophie's problem seems to have taken him out of this latest funk, jerked him back to life somehow. And let me tell you, Meredith, I don't need him looking over my shoulder all day long, watching everything I do. That's bad enough. But if he should ever figure out that I—"

"God, Graham, but you've got a big mouth," Meredith said, cutting him off. "There's a billboard on the way to Prosperino. A big one, with lights and these little slats that turn around to show two different ads. You might want to rent it. One side could say 'I did it!' and the other could tell the whole damn world exactly what it is that you did."

"All right, all right, I get your point," Graham said. "We'll drop the subject." There was a short silence. "Would you look at this place? There must be over two hundred presents in here. What a bunch of ass-kissers sucking up to good old Senator Joe. It's going to cost me a small fortune to top any of these gifts."

"You worry about the damnedest things, Graham," Meredith said, her voice dripping with a sarcasm that sent a shiver down Sophie's spine. "Write a check to the Hopechest Ranch. You know how he gets all soppy about those misfit brats. That will make him all gooey and thankful to you."

"Good point, Meredith," Graham agreed. "And he'd never know the amount, because they don't give out that sort of information. Do they?"

Meredith laughed, and it wasn't a pleasant sound. "I wouldn't bet on it, Graham. I think you're going to have to ante up at least five grand. Oh, and you're late with this month's check, you know. For a man who worries so much about being discovered, you're strangely slow to pay your bills."

As their voices were getting quieter, coming to her from farther away, Sophie opened the door slightly and peered inside. She was just in time to see a rectangular piece of paper change hands, from Graham to Meredith, as the two of them walked toward the door leading to the hallway.

"Did you ever hear that old saying, Graham?" Meredith was asking him as she pocketed the check. "The one that says two people can keep a secret if one of them is dead?"

"If you're saying I should kill you, Meredith,"

Graham Colton grumbled, hands stuck deep in his pockets, "don't think it's never occurred to me."

Meredith threw back her head and laughed. Rather maniacally. "You don't have the guts, Graham. You never did."

And then they were gone, the door to the room closed behind them. Sophie came back into the room and headed for the nearest chair, her knees weak.

That was her *mother?* That awful, terrible, crude, grasping woman was her *mother?*

And her uncle Graham? What was that all about? What secret did the two of them share? Why was money changing hands? What in *hell* was happening?

Sophie couldn't go to her father. She just couldn't. She couldn't do anything more than repeat what she'd heard, and what she'd heard hadn't made any sense.

She could go to River. No. No, that wouldn't be a good idea. River already disliked her uncle, for one thing, and she was reluctant to carry yet another tale about her mother, her mother's strange behavior.

Which left Sophie to her own counsel or, as it stood now, completely at sea, because she hadn't the faintest idea what was going on, what her mother and her uncle Graham had been discussing.

"But I can't let this go. I just can't," Sophie told herself, heading outside once more, picking up the boxes to carry them to the recycling bins. "After the party. It's only a few days away now anyway. After the party I'll get River, maybe Rand and Drake, and all of us can talk to Dad, somehow convince him that Mom has to go somewhere, get some professional help. We just need to get past this damn party."

* * *

River had his head down as he sat on the bench outside the stable door, concentrating on what he was doing, so that he didn't hear Rand's approach until his foster brother said hello.

"A swan? Is that a swan?" Rand then asked, pointing to the large bar of soap River was carefully whittling with his pocket knife. "Sure it is. Amazing, Riv. That's very good."

"Thanks," River said, carefully drawing the knife along the swan's thin, curving neck, then setting the carving aside. He was at the most delicate part of the carving and didn't want to make a mistake because he wasn't giving the work his full concentration. He hoped Rand wasn't planning on staying long, because he wanted to have the swan done and on Sophie's bed before dinnertime. "You've been here a lot lately. A few weeks ago, and now again. I hope you're getting frequent flyer miles from here to D.C."

"I may work out of D.C., but I just can't seem to keep my practice from being bi-coastal. I never really left California after I was here last, actually. Doing some work for Dad, checking up on matters for a client in Los Angeles, another in Sacramento. I could have gone back to Washington, I suppose, but with the party coming up so soon, I figured, why bother? I'll be staying out here until after Dad's birthday. So, how are you doing? How's the house and everything coming along?"

"Fine. Fine." River stood up, closed the knife and stuck it into the pocket of his jeans. "Planning on a ride?'' he asked, looking at Rand's outfit of plaid shirt, worn jeans and cowboy boots.

Rand laughed softly. "Looks like it, doesn't it? But no. I was cleaning up the small office I use when I'm out here, and figured I should dress for the part, then figured I might as well hang on to the urban cowboy look, as I was driving up here anyway. I have a cleaning service, but nothing gets dustier than law books, and the service doesn't seem to do more than give them an occasional swipe with a dust rag.''

River grinned. "They brought us up right, didn't they, Rand? Don't ask anyone to do anything for you unless you also can and are willing to do it for yourself.''

"Yeah, that just about sums it up, I guess,'' Rand said, shrugging his broad shoulders. Rand was a big man, over six feet, with dark hair and deep blue eyes—a close likeness to photographs of Joe at the same age. That was probably why River so instinctively trusted him, was proud to have him as a friend. "Too bad. Because I was just going to offer to do something for you that you probably should do for yourself.''

"Oh?'' River asked, heading for the small refrigerator just inside the stable, planning on getting them each a bottle of ice water. "What were you going to do for me that I should do for myself?''

Rand's smile was self-conscious as well as teasing. "Tell Sophie that you love her. That swan's for her, isn't it? The swan, the book, the rock candy. Inez loves to talk, River, and then Maya talks to Drake. We've got this really great early-warning system, us

Coltons, and news travels faster than the speed of
light. If I were in D.C. rather than here, I'd probably
have a stack of faxes from Drake by now. They really
have to get that boy back on active duty, before he
turns into a gossip columnist. So, does she know?''

"That I love her? Sure, she knows,'' River told
him, walking back over to Rand and handing him one
of the bottles. "I'm just giving her time to start to
believe it. I spent a lot of years pushing her away,
you know. Too many years. I almost lost her.''

Rand shook his head. "You never lost her. Remember, River, I'm the one she came to, to talk about
our friend Chet Wallace. She flew all the way to
Washington to talk to me. She never loved him. It
was going to be a business partnership, pure and simple. Maybe the engagement was also meant to wake
you up, shake you up. I can't be sure of that, and I
doubt if Sophie knows herself. I do know she was
more than ready to call it off with Chet, quit her job
and come back here to write a book. The fact that
you're here probably didn't have much to do with it.
It wouldn't have been more than, say, ninety-nine percent of the reason.''

River scratched at the back of his neck, then neatly
slipped his hand higher, to push at the brim of his
cowboy hat and tip it lower over his eyes. "You think
so?''

"I think so,'' Rand said, then laughed. "Excuse
me, but are you really River James, or are you just
impersonating him? Because the Riv I know would
have stomped up that hill long ago, tossed my sister
over his shoulder and plunked her down somewhere

until she listened to him. Swans? You're giving her *swans?* God, Riv, that's so lovesick and pathetic.''

"Great. Now I'm getting romantic advice from the self-acknowledged playboy of the western world. Lucky me. Back off, Rand, all right?''

Rand held up his hands in surrender. ''You got it. But I had to tease you, Riv. Sophie's my sister. It's like I'm honor bound to make your life a living hell.''

River grinned. ''Trust me on this one thing, Rand. Your stubborn sister doesn't need any help in making my life a living hell. But not for long. Tell you what—I'll even give you a timetable, so you can be sure to watch. By the time Joe lifts his glass when we toast his sixtieth birthday, Sophie will have agreed to marry me.''

"Well, I'll drink to that right now!'' Rand said, lifting the bottled water to his mouth, then holding it there as he turned his head, and frowned at the car that drove toward the house. ''What's he doing here?''

River looked at the car as it disappeared up the drive, then at Rand, who had gone rather white and tight around the mouth. ''Emmett Fallon? Why shouldn't he be here? Maybe he has to talk to Joe about something going on at the office.''

Rand gave a wave of his hand. ''Never mind. After all, it's not like I can put my finger on any one thing, can say—see, *that's* why I don't trust him. But I don't, River. And the older I get and the more I see, the less I trust him. He's envious of Dad, believes he should have a bigger piece of the profits. I think he'd yank out Dad's eyeteeth, if he could get a good grip on them.''

"So Emmett's not you favorite guy, huh?'' Rand wouldn't be here long, only until after the party, so River decided to talk to him while he could.

"You mean Uncle Marry-a-lot and his wife, my aunt Jeannie, no Sarah, no Beth Ann, no—Doris. That's the wife of the week, isn't it? Doris?''

"That's it? The playboy of the western world is disenchanted with his courtesy uncle because he marries the women he sleeps with?'' River asked, then took a long drink of water. "There's got to be more to it than that.''

"Oh, there is, Riv, there is. I've been out in the big, bad world long enough to recognize a sycophant when I see one. Kissing Dad's boots, playing loyal friend and employee—and all the while hating his guts. And Uncle Graham is even worse. You know, Dad used to live in D.C. when he was a kid, so I've done a little snooping around, asked a few questions, learned a few things about his parents, about dearest Uncle Graham.''

"Really?'' River said, taking up his seat on the bench once more, ready to listen to whatever Rand had to say, about Fallon, about Graham Colton.

"Yes, really,'' Rand answered with a smile. "And now you're going to sit there, real quiet, and wait for me to spill my guts, right?''

"If it works…'' River said, shrugging.

"Okay, but I'm only going to give you the short version. Dad's father, Teddy, was a lawyer in Washington. Not a good one, but he loved to party, so he had a lot of friends. He married my grandmother, Kay, who had money but not the same social background Teddy had. It was a trade-off for him, I guess, as he'd always wanted the money to live as he thought his supposedly impeccable lineage deserved.''

"There's always a lot of that going around," River said, tongue in cheek.

"How true! Anyway, Teddy and Kay begat Joe, and then Graham five years later—Teddy obviously a man who didn't know to quit while he was ahead. A few years after that, Teddy, who liked to drink, took Kay, who also liked to drink, and plowed the two of them into a tree one night on the way home from a party. Orphaned, young Joe and Graham went to live with mommy's rich parents. Only mommy's rich parents didn't like Joe, because Joe looked too much like his drunken daddy who had killed their little girl. So they shipped Joe out here, to live with Teddy's old army buddy, Jack McGrath."

River held up a hand to stop Rand's recitation. "I know that part. Joe felt like he'd been abandoned, banished, but it turned out to be the best thing that could have happened to him. Jack and Maureen McGrath took him in, even though they had a bunch of kids of their own and not a lot of money, and, to hear Joe tell it, made a man out of him. That's one of the reasons I got to be here, because Joe wanted to give something back, take in foster kids of his own. But I don't know Graham's story."

Rand drank the rest of his water, crushed the plastic bottle and tossed it into a nearby can. "Poor Graham.

And poor Ed and Betty—Kay's doting parents. One, they kept the wrong kid, because Graham may have looked like Kay, but he was Teddy, through and through. Add to that the fact that old Ed and Betty eventually lost all their money, and you've got a recipe for Graham showing up on the now wealthy Joe's doorstep after years of very little communication, saying, 'Hi, bro, what do you say we bond, and all that good stuff?'"

"To which Joe, being Joe," River concluded, "said, 'Sure, you got it. Anything that's mine is yours, little brother.' Right?"

"Right," Rand said, his lips twisting into a grimace. "Just the way he said it to Emmett Fallon, just because they went into one small mining project together. Now Emmett thinks he deserves a bite from every slice of pie that makes up Colton Enterprises. The mines, the media, you name it. If my dad has a fault, River, it's that he's too damn good, too damn nice, and *way* too damn trusting."

"I watch him," River said, standing up, tossing his own empty bottle into the trash can. "We all do, all of us who are still here. You can count on that, Rand."

"I do, Riv," Rand said, putting an arm around his foster brother's shoulder for a moment, giving River a quick, affectionate squeeze. "That's why I dump on you, old friend, and why I'm rooting for you to become my brother-in-law. You'll work on that, right?"

"I'm always working on that, Rand," River said, and then returned to the bench and picked up the swan that still needed some finishing touches. Rand left him there, saying he would walk back up to the house, to drop in on Joe, to make sure Emmett Fallon wasn't saying anything too stupid.

Nodding, River pulled the knife from his pocket opened it, and started to whittle. The swan would be good, all his presents would be good, and then the day of the party would be upon them. Joe's party, his sixtieth birthday, and the beginning, River hoped, of a whole new happiness for Sophie and himself.

It was going to be one hell of a night, one they'd never forget.

Sixteen

The day of the party dawned bright and sunny, and wonderfully "California," so that everyone relaxed, not that anyone except Inez had been really worried about the possibility of rain. After all, the weather wouldn't dare to ruin such an important party.

The large house was already crammed to the rafters with Coltons, and Inez had given up trying to do anything more than put out huge buffets three times a day, then wave anyone out of the kitchens with a sturdy wooden spoon if they dared to invade her sanctuary between meals. Nora Hickman, the kitchen helper, had even taken to working round the clock, right alongside Inez.

The entire courtyard and gardens had been strung with tiny white fairy lights; there were three huge tents set up on the lawns. The fountain had been scrubbed until it glistened, and the florist had actually done the impossible—he'd improved the looks of the courtyard with potted plants and masses of flowers.

There was a portable stage inside the huge living room for one live band, and another in the courtyard, which would be used for yet another band and also to serve as a podium for what would surely be more than one speaker who wished to toast the birthday boy.

Joe's wonderfully eccentric Aunt Sybil, who had arrived from Paris a day earlier, had pestered Sophie until she unearthed some ashtrays to set around. The eighty-eight-year-old Sybil had declared that either she'd be allowed to indulge her vice or she'd be on the next jet back to Europe. "After all, if it weren't for sex and cigarettes, I'd have nothing to live for at all," the old woman had said, naughtily winking at Sophie.

Sophie found the ashtrays. She also checked with Marco to make sure there were freshly cut flowers in all the bedrooms—Meredith's orders to the florist not extending to any niceties for anyone save herself. Finally, she made arrangements to have a meal set out in the kitchen for all the reporters and photographers who would be covering the party, as Meredith hadn't made any such provision for the last large party, which had been, in Sophie's opinion, a glaring oversight.

So everything was done. Everything was ready. Inez had outdone herself, spending nearly two days on the huge birthday cake that would, conservatively, serve more than three hundred people. The catering trucks had arrived, Sophie could hear chairs being opened and set up in small groupings in the courtyard, under the tents. Her father was already complaining about having to wear a tuxedo, and Meredith had been locked in her room for the past three hours with her hairdresser and a makeup artist he'd brought with him from the salon.

Two more hours, and the party would be in full swing. Six more hours, and it would all be over. All the work, the preparation, the hustle and the bustle— and it would be over.

What then? What would happen when it was over, and everyone said goodbye and went back to their own lives? Rand back to Washington. Drake to be gone soon, off to some place he couldn't name to do some thing he couldn't discuss. Amber had already announced that she'd be leaving for a trip with friends the morning after the party.

Emily would stay, of course. And Rebecca would visit from time to time. As for the rest of the foster children Joe and Meredith had taken in over the years? Well, Chance would go back on the road, selling farm equipment and running as far and as fast as he could from the legacy of his abusive father. Tripp, now a pediatrician, certainly couldn't stay away from his busy practice. Wyatt would go back to Washington with Rand, as they were lawyers in the same firm. Even Blake Fallon, Emmett's son, once so troubled that he came to live at the ranch for a while, would probably only be able to stop in about once a week, as he was so very busy running Hopechest Ranch.

Leaving, Sophie knew, River James.

River wasn't going anywhere. He'd move to his own place soon, but that was only a short ride away from the house, from Sophie, who also wasn't going anywhere.

Unless Sophie took her aunt Sybil up on her offer to go back to Paris with her for a few months. It would be a nice place to start writing her book, the one she planned about the history of Hopechest Ranch. All things considered, it was a tempting offer.

What would River do if she left the country? Would he try to stop her from leaving? He never had before.

"Flowers, Sophie," Maya Ramirez said, knocking on Sophie's bedroom door, then walking in, hidden behind at least three dozen long-stemmed red roses.

"Good God, Maya!" Sophie exclaimed, taking the heavy vase from Inez's daughter. "Your father grew these?"

Maya's exotic dark eyes shone with amusement. "He's good, Sophie, but not that good. Besides, if he ever grew roses like these, he'd threaten us all with a hedge clipper before he'd allow them to be cut. There's a card," she said, pointing to a small white card tucked in with the blooms. "Well, gotta go. Mom is having a nervous breakdown, which means that everything's just perfect and she has nothing else to do but worry between now and tonight. Don't forget, Soph, there's still that private dinner party at six, for the VIP-est of the VIPs, before everyone else shows up. Senator Howard is already here, and he and your dad have broken into that box of cigars Representative Blakely gave him as a gift. Mom's going wild, saying they're stinking up the house.''

"Mmm, hmm," Sophie responded absently, putting the heavy vase on the center of her dresser, then reaching for the card. The envelope had her name printed on it, and when she pulled out the card inside, there was more printing. Simple, short, and to the point: ''You asked what's upstairs. Come see.''

"Now?" Sophie asked, looking at the card. "He stays away all this time, sending me presents, and he picks *now?*"

A slow smile started on Sophie's face, and quickly grew into a grin. She could do it. She had time. She'd been given clearance to drive. She'd already had her shower, she was ready to get dressed. Inez would perform her miracles without her. She could do this. She *would* do this.

"Damn you, River James," Sophie said, pulling a simple black full-length sheath over her head, shaking her head to rearrange her well-cut hair. She applied lipstick, too nervous to do more than that, and gave her scar a quick look, knowing she should get out her makeup, cover it up. "Oh, who cares?" she said, grinning at her reflection. She didn't care. All of a sudden, for no reason she could explain, even to herself, she just didn't care. "If they don't like it, they damn well don't have to look!"

"Sophie, Aunt Sybil says there still aren't ashtrays outside. What should I do?" Emily called to her as Sophie ran through the living room in her high heels.

"Tell her to take up chewing tobacco, and then she can just spit in the flower pots!" Sophie happily called back over her shoulder, snagging the SUV keys from the hook just inside the front door.

"*Chew?* But—but—" Emily said, taking two steps toward Sophie, who was already gone, racing out to the SUV. Moments later, the tires scattered gravel as Sophie took off down the drive.

"We're not getting anywhere, are we?" Louise Smith asked, sighing. "We know my grandmother's name was Sophie. We know I think I saw myself in that other garden—*two* of myself—although how that's possible is anyone's guess. And now you tell me we're going to have to back off and not use hypnosis again for a while. Why?"

Dr. Wilkes put down the clipboard she used to take notes during sessions, and looked at Louise levelly. "Why, Louise? You know why. The headaches. These debilitating migraines you've been getting."

"I've had the headaches as long as I can remember," Louise reasoned.

"Yes, but not almost nightly. I'm glad your doctor prescribed medication, but that medication is strong stuff, and I don't want to think about you having all those chemicals on board while I'm taking peeks inside your mind. You're losing more weight, you're telling me that the nightmares are getting worse. No, I can't do it, Louise. Not as your psychologist, not as your friend. We're going to back off, just for a little while, just until we get these migraines under control."

Louise blinked back tears. "I had so wanted to see that little girl again," she said, sighing. "But I—

Patsy—keeps pushing her away, out of the frame. That's what it's like, you know. Like a movie I'm seeing. I'm there, in the picture, but I'm also watching from a distance. The audience.'' She shook her head. ''I do so miss that little girl.''

River watched from the bedroom window as the SUV appeared in the distance, then slowly walked down the steps, doing his best to pretend he was calm, that his heart wasn't racing inside his chest, that his palms weren't damp, that his stomach wasn't tied in knots.

He raised a hand to the black silk bow tie at his neck, the contraption it had taken him twenty frustrating minutes to construct, then swallowed down hard. The last time he'd worn a monkey suit had been the night of Sophie's prom. He'd worn a rented tux and a string tie, and his rented patent leather shoes had squeaked when he walked.

Now he owned his own tux, his own black onyx studs, and for the price he'd paid for his shoes, if they squeaked he'd have somebody's head. Personally, he thought the snow-white shirt with conventional collar and minutely pleated front looked pretty good against his tanned skin, although he had debated for long moments before finally tying back his hair with a thin strip of black material he'd braided out of the extra material left over from the alterations on the tux.

He wasn't Chet Wallace. He didn't want to be Chet Wallace. But he didn't feel like he'd spend the whole night wishing himself out of the tux, back in his jeans and cowboy boots.

River heard the car door close, silently counted to ten, and then opened the front door just as Sophie was approaching the front porch. "You look beautiful, Soph," he said, waiting for her to raise her head as she carefully lifted her hem and stepped up onto the porch.

"I look like I got dressed in five minutes flat, which I did." She kept her head down a moment longer, then raised her eyes to look at him. "My God," she said, taking an involuntary step backward. "You... you look..." She shook her head. "My God."

"That bad?"

She pressed her lips together and shook her head. She took in a deep breath and let it out slowly. "You have to be illegal in at least three states," she said at last, and then she smiled. "I liked the swan best," she told him. "I liked it best because you carved it yourself. You did, didn't you?"

He nodded and held out his hand. "Come inside. Come upstairs with me."

"I thought you'd never ask." She took his hand, then preceded him into the house.

Meredith turned her head left, then right, then looked into the mirror over her dressing table to see the reflection coming from the large hand mirror Frank held up so that she could see the intricate twists and curls he had magically woven into her upswept hairstyle. "Perfect. It's just perfect, Frank," she told him enthusiastically. "You're a genius."

"It helps that I have a great subject to work with,

Mrs. Colton,'' the hairdresser said, stowing the hand mirror in a side pocket of the large canvas bag he'd brought with him from his salon. "Now don't you worry about those curls falling. I've sprayed them within an inch of their lives, although they won't feel hard or stiff. Here," he said, putting the hair spray canister on the dressing table, "I'll leave this for you. You're really going to love it."

"Thank you, Frank," Meredith said, standing up, unsnapping the leopard skin silk smock Frank had brought with him to cover her gown. The action revealed a bright pink and green patterned gown—the print almost tropical—floor-length and split in the front to Meredith's knees, the bodice also spilt, nearly to her navel. The fact that the gown was long-sleeved only served to make her bodice look more exposed, more bare.

She turned back to the dressing table and picked up a diamond-and-gold necklace Joe had given his wife on their twentieth anniversary, handing it to Frank so that he would clasp it behind her neck, then slipped diamond teardrops—each a full carat—into her ears. "Too much?" she asked, spreading her arms and doing a quick pirouette.

Frank reached forward to give a slight tug to one of the long, curling wisps that framed Meredith's face. "Perfect. I wouldn't change a thing."

"I would," Meredith said, smiling wickedly. "I'd make the diamonds bigger." Then she laughed, extracted a few hundred-dollar bills from the top drawer of her dressing table and approached Frank, brushing her body against his as she stuffed the bills into his shirt pocket. "Now run along. I have to be bored at dinner in a little while, and I think I'll spend the next few minutes pouring martinis down my throat, to prepare."

Frank laughed, as he was supposed to do, and quickly gathered up the rest of his equipment. He motioned for the makeup artist, who had been amusing herself filing her cherry-tipped nails, to follow him, and soon Meredith was alone.

She wanted to be alone, needed to be alone. She reached into the top drawer of her dressing table one more time, extracting a short, thin glass vial with a tiny screw-off top. The vial was half filled with a clear liquid.

"Damn gown," she said, patting at her hips. "Where in hell am I going to hide this thing?" She looked down at herself, how she'd been so cunningly lifted and all but glued to the gown in order to accommodate her plunging neckline. "You can't tuck it in the usual place, because you aren't wearing the original place, are you, Meredith?" she asked herself, longing for a drink, but needing to settle this last problem before she could allow her mind to be even the least bit clouded.

"Can't carry a purse," she said, talking to herself. "Why would a hostess carry a purse to her own party? And I can't take the chance I'll have time to come back here without missing the toast. Damn! There has to be someplace I can—" she cut herself off, looked at the can of hair spray.

Would it work? Was it possible? Frank had said nothing could disturb her hair, make any of the real or fake curls fall. Meredith sat down in front of the mirror, gathered up the few hairpins Frank had left scattered on the top of the dressing table. Carefully, she lifted one large sculpted curl and slid the bottle into her teased hair, then secured the curl again with three nearly invisible hairpins.

She looked at her reflection, noticed nothing out of the ordinary and picked up the can of hair spray and misted it over her head. She waited, shook her head and shook her head again.

"Oh, yes, Frank, you were right. I most certainly *do* love this hair spray!" she said, then went in search of a drink.

"I still can't believe you did this," Sophie said, looking around the bedroom from her vantage point— which happened to be the middle of the king-size bed she and River had just made such very good use of a few minutes earlier.

River propped himself up on one elbow and also looked at the room. Random planked hardwood floors, palest green wallpaper, sheer white curtains. A bedroom set made up of an antique cherry dresser he'd found in Prosperino, a chest of drawers with double doors that he'd finished himself, a glass-and-brass dressing table he had been pretty sure Sophie would like and, of course, that all-important king-size bed with its snow-white comforter dotted with bunches of wildflowers.

"You like it?"

"No, I hate it," Sophie said, pulling a face as she gave him a push, knocking his arm out from under him. "How could I *not* like it? Did you ever stop to think that this whole room might constitute a bribe? That I'm only here in bed with you because I love this room?"

"You wouldn't accept your weight in diamonds if you didn't want the man who came with them," River said, tracing a fingertip down her upper arm. "Besides, it wasn't the room that did it. It was the swan, remember?"

"No ugly ducklings, only swans," Sophie said, snuggling back against the pillows, taking his hand in her own. "Tell me you love me."

"You love me," River teased, then quickly grabbed Sophie's arms so that she couldn't attack him. He leaned over her, his head close to hers. "You love me," he repeated. "I love you. I will love you for the next million years."

Sophie raised a hand to his cheek. "I still don't believe it. All the wrong turns, all the wrong words, all the stupid mistakes—"

"This would be *you* you're talking about, right?" River interrupted, dropping a kiss on her nose. "Because I'm perfect. As a matter of fact, I think you even said so a little while ago."

"Never believe anything I say in the heat of passion," Sophie warned, grinning. "But I know what you're doing, Riv. You want us both to forget what happened, and to start thinking about the future. Am I right?"

"I wouldn't forget a moment of our lives, Sophie," River corrected, his voice low, almost a whisper. "But I admit I do prefer to remember the good times more than the bad. Besides, everything we said or did or failed to say or do brought us to this point. There can't be anything bad about that, right?''

''You're brilliant,'' Sophie told him, reaching up to nip at his chin.

''I am? Are you in the heat of passion? Because, if you are, I think I can probably accommodate you.''

''Idiot!'' Sophie said, laughing, and then she sobered. ''Are you ever going to ask, Riv?''

He was busy nuzzling the side of her neck. ''Ask? Ask what?''

Sophie closed her eyes, felt herself melting again, her mind getting wonderfully muzzy. ''About the pregnancy test, of course. I did take one...or two. Don't you want to know?''

''Nope,'' he said, reluctantly moving away from her. ''And do you know why? I don't want to know because it makes no difference. I love you and I want to marry you. I want to marry you tomorrow, tonight. If we have one baby, or ten babies, or no babies, it doesn't change that, Soph. I love you.''

''Oh, Riv, you're something else,'' Sophie told him, blinking back tears. ''And I believe you. I believe you, and I love you. So I might as well tell you whether you ask or not. I took the test, and I'm definitely—''

River put two fingers over her mouth as he slowly shook his head. ''Later,'' he said, then waited until she nodded her agreement before removing his fingers and replacing them with his mouth.

River and Sophie never did get to the private family dinner party, arriving back at the ranch only after making love yet again, then spending ten minutes on their hands and knees on the bedroom floor, looking for two missing black onyx shirt studs.

"You're late," Rand said, sidling up to River as he stood in front of one of the portable bars set up in the courtyard. "I bet Drake five bucks you and Sophie would announce your engagement tonight. Am I going to be right?"

"Should have made it ten," River said, grinning as he turned away from the bar, a glass of beer in one hand, a safe glass of ginger ale in the other, because he was pretty sure there was no milk at the bar. Besides, Sophie had said she wanted them to keep her pregnancy a secret between just the two of them for a little while longer. Not too much longer, River knew, because otherwise he was probably going to explode with the joy of their secret—that the lone wolf wasn't going to be alone for long, that he had a mate now, that he and his mate would soon be a family. "We're going to wait until after the birthday toasts, then tell everyone that we're going to be married."

"Good," Rand said, giving River a hearty slap on the back, so that he nearly spilled his beer. "I knew I could count on you, Riv. Congratulations!"

Sophie stood next to Jackson Colton, Graham's son and her cousin, and watched the increased activity around the base of the outdoor stage. The night sky was speckled with bright stars, the air was comfortably cool and the courtyard was a veritable mass of tuxedos and sophisticated black gowns and sparkling jewels.

"She really stands out in that gown, doesn't she?" Jackson asked, using his wineglass to point toward Meredith.

"Yes," Sophie agreed. "I think she planned it that way." She watched as Meredith raised a hand to her hair, patting at the mass of curls rather nervously. Did she have a headache? Sophie felt she should go to her, see if she was all right, but then Cheyenne James joined them and the conversation drifted in another direction.

"My brother is looking rather extraordinarily handsome this evening," Cheyenne said, winking at Jackson. "There's this sort of glow about River tonight, don't you think? Rather like the one Sophie is wearing."

Jackson looked at Sophie and frowned. "Am I missing something here?" he asked, and both women laughed as River joined them, carrying a small plate of cocktail shrimp he handed to Sophie.

"Hi, little sis," River said, kissing Cheyenne's cheek. "What's so funny?"

"You," Cheyenne teased, kissing him back. "And don't think you can keep secrets from me, Riv, because you know you can't. I'm psychic, you know." Then she turned to Jackson. "Do you think we could go scare up a couple of drinks? I'm dying of thirst. Oh, there's Rebecca. I need to talk to her about something. Be sweet, Jackson, and find me a cold drink, with lots of ice. I'll be over there, with Rebecca."

"Why is it I keep letting women boss me around?"

Jackson said as Cheyenne walked off, her waist-length, jet black hair swaying as she moved. "Nice girl, your sister," he added. "We've been talking almost nonstop, as a matter of fact, except for when she runs off to talk to somebody else. Why haven't I met her before tonight?"

"Because you're too busy working twenty-six hours a day, protecting Colton Enterprises," Sophie said, laughing at Jackson's perplexed look. "And she wasn't kidding, you know. Cheyenne *is* psychic. Isn't she, Riv?"

"When she lets herself be, yes," River said, and Jackson peered after Cheyenne once more, but she had disappeared into the crowd milling in the courtyard.

"Well, if she's psychic, she'll know I'm going to do as she said and go find us something cold to drink, especially since it looks like the toasts are about to begin. I think I'll use the service entrance and raid Joe's private stock in his study. There'll be less of a crowd that way. I'll catch you two later, okay?"

Jackson walked off, and River took Sophie's hand and eased them both closer to the stage, so they'd have a better view of the toasts. "Your mother looks—is the right word *spectacular?*"

Sophie stood on tiptoe, trying to catch a glimpse of her mother, but all she could see was Emmett Fallon, who came at her so suddenly out of the crowd that he nearly ran her down.

"Oh, sorry, Sophie," Emmett said, wearing a designer tux and his usual frown. "Didn't see you. I've got to scare up a drink before the toasts." And then he was gone, heading toward the house, just as Jackson had done.

"Jackass," River muttered under his breath. "Are you all right, little mother?"

"Oh, I'm fine, unless you think you're going to call me little mother for the next eight months, in which case *you* aren't going to be fine," she answered with a grin, going up on tiptoe to kiss his cheek. "What a madhouse. Mom invited the whole world. Look, Riv, Dad's climbing up on the stage, bringing Mom with him. Do you think he's going to make a speech?"

"Sure looks like it. Your mother's got two champagne glasses. Here, let's get closer so you can see."

Somehow, River maneuvered them closer to the stage, so that Sophie could see her mother standing in the glow from the spotlights directed at the stage. She looked beautiful as she handed one champagne glass to her husband. Young, happy, without a care in the world. Sophie watched as Meredith lifted a hand to her hair, patting her curls, smiling as if she knew how beautiful she looked.

"Speech! Speech!" someone yelled from the crowd, and the chant was taken up, growing louder until Joe held out his hands and asked for quiet.

"Thank you," Joe said, and Sophie blinked back happy tears as she watched and listened to her father. He made a small joke at his own expense, then became serious for a moment, thanking everyone for coming, for reminding him that he wasn't "just an old warhorse gone out to pasture, but an old warhorse with a lot of friends and a lot of living still to do."

"Hear, hear!" someone yelled, and Sophie turned to smile at Rand, who winked at her. "Sixty more, Dad! Sixty more!"

Joe laughed, pointed at his firstborn son. "I'll drink to that!" he exclaimed, raising the champagne flute to his lips.

Sophie was just raising her own glass, smiling at River, thinking that he'd make as wonderful a father as her own dad was to her, when a loud shot rang out. She turned, instinctively, in time to see her father going down. His arm around Meredith, his body shielding hers or leaning on hers, Joe Colton crashed to the stage, out of Sophie's line of sight.

"Daddy!" she yelled as River took her hand and pushed through the panicked, shouting crowd of guests, heading toward the stage. *"Daddy!"*

In Mississippi, in a small bedroom shrouded in darkness, Louise Smith sat up, pressed trembling hands to her cheeks and screamed.

She screamed...and she screamed...and she screamed.

* * * * *

Don't miss the continuation
of the Colton family saga
with Linda Turner's
THE VIRGIN MISTRESS.

One

The Colton estate near Prosperino, California, was called the Hacienda del Alegria—the House of Joy— and it gave every appearance of being just that. Situated in a beautiful valley, the large sand-colored adobe house faced the mountains in the distance and backed up to the ocean, offering spectacular views from every direction.

As a child, Austin had loved coming there. There was the ranch to explore, as well as the ocean, and then there was the house, itself. Built in a V-shape, with two wings that jutted off the main section, it was a home, not just a house, thanks to Meredith. Back then, she'd had no interest in being a society queen, just a wife and mother, and she'd made sure the house was comfortably decorated and filled with children. She'd even done much of the gardening around the main house herself, and in the process, she'd created a lush tropical paradise that everyone had loved.

It had been years since Austin had been there, but the minute he drove down the lane to the house, he could see that it wasn't the same as he remembered from his childhood. Oh, the house was the same structurally, but the grounds were professionally landscaped now and had lost that wild, natural look they'd always had when Meredith tended them herself. Now the place looked just like any other rich man's estate.

And so did the house, itself. The second the maid, Inez, who had been with the family as long as Austin could remember, opened the door for him, he could see that this wasn't the home he'd always enjoyed visiting when he was a child. It was more formal. In a single glance, Austin noted the expensive decor that had replaced the once comfortable furnishings that had made the house so welcoming in the past. The inviting home he remembered now appeared to be just a showcase for the Colton wealth. And that was a shame.

When he greeted Inez, however, none of his thoughts were reflected in his smile. "It's been a long time, Inez. I don't have to ask if Marco's been taking care of you. You look wonderful."

At the mention of her husband, who was the head groundskeeper, her pretty black eyes twinkled merrily. "Marco's a smart man," she replied. "He knows I'm the best thing that ever happened to him. You're looking good, too." Sobering, she confided, "Mr. Joe will be glad you're here. These last few days haven't been easy for him."

"No, I don't imagine they have. I'll need to talk to you later about that, okay?"

"Any time, Mr. Austin. I was just about to start supper. You're family. You know the way, right?"

It had been years, but Austin could have found Joe's study blindfolded in the dark. "Sure. Thanks."

Located down the hall from the living room, the study was decorated just as Austin remembered—with a huge oak desk and big, comfortable leather chairs, and books everywhere. Pleased that that much had stayed the same, at least, Austin grinned at the sight of his uncle scowling at his computer screen. It had been years since he'd seen him but he was still one good-looking son of a gun. At sixty, he was strong and athletic in spite of the gray that peppered his dark brown hair.

"Watch it, unc," he teased. "Frowning like that's going to cause wrinkles if you're not careful."

"Austin! Thank God! Just the man I wanted to see." Grinning broadly, he jumped up from his chair and strode around his desk to envelop him in a bear hug. "I made some notes of the shooting and was just going over them. I keep thinking if I read them enough, I'll figure out who the hell tried to kill me."

That sounded good, but Austin knew better than to think it would be that easy. Someone had come damn close to pulling off a murder in full view of an entire party of birthday guests without anyone seeing him—or her. Which meant this wasn't a crime of passion. It had been plotted and planned down to the smallest detail by someone who didn't lack for cleverness or daring. Cracking it wasn't going to be easy.

Nodding at the computer screen and Joe's notes as he sank into one of the chairs in front of his desk, he said, "I'd like to have a copy of that and the guest list. I'll need to talk to everyone who was here that night."

"I've got it all right here," his uncle said, handing him the information he'd already printed out for him. "The police needed the same thing, not that they did much with it," he added in disgust. "They still keep insisting it's someone in the family."

Not surprised, Austin said, "You can't really blame them, Joe. Think about it. Somebody tried to kill you at your own birthday party. There were no enemies here at the house that day—at least not that you know of. Just friends and family. And a shot was fired from the crowd. It's only logical that the police suspect the family. Who else has the most to gain from your death and was present when the shot was fired?"

Not liking that one little bit, Joe growled, "Are you saying you agree with the police? I need to be suspicious of my own family?"

He gave him a look that had, no doubt, made lesser men quake in their shoes, but Austin didn't so much as blink. Joe had called him down to Prosperino to do a job, and he intended to do it—even when that meant telling him something he didn't want to hear.

"I won't know that until I examine the facts and talk to the witnesses," he said honestly. "Only time will tell. For your sake, I hope the shooter's not someone in the family, but if that's who it turns out to be, you'll have to deal with it. You could end up dead if you don't."

*   *   *   *   *